Carolyn Friesen is a single mother of two young adults. She loves to be with them and spend quality time with each other. She enjoys history, historical reenactments, and museums. She spends time researching history and finding stories that have often been forgotten. In the winter, she flies to warmer climates to get away from the bitter Canadian cold. She is a believer in Jesus Christ and puts her trust in him.

This book is dedicated to my sister, Audrey. Her upbeat enthusiasm and her positive encouragement gave me courage when writing was a challenge.

Carolyn Friesen

BELLA

AUSTIN MACAULEY PUBLISHERS™

LONDON • CAMBRIDGE • NEW YORK • SHARJAH

Ordering Information
Quantity sales: Special discounts are available on quantity purchases by corporations, associations, and others. For details, contact the publisher at the address below.

Publisher's Cataloging-in-Publication data
Friesen, Carolyn
Bella

ISBN 9798886936049 (Paperback)
ISBN 9798886936056 (ePub e-book)

Library of Congress Control Number: 2024908147

www.austinmacauley.com/us

First Published 2024
Austin Macauley Publishers LLC
40 Wall Street, 33rd Floor, Suite 3302
New York, NY 10005
USA

mail-usa@austinmacauley.com
+1 (646) 5125767

Chapter 1

The gentle breeze teased my hair piled loosely atop my head, as I sat under the ancient oak in front of my home that I shared with my chosen parents. Brushing the wisps of hair that framed my face out of my blue eyes, the warm sun rays made me sleepy and I closed my eyes, my dark lashes brushing my cheeks.

I was studying for my teacher's certificate, hoping to start teaching in early autumn. My grades were excellent and I hoped that it wouldn't be a problem to get into a school.

My thoughts wandered as I pondered on my chosen profession, recalling my school days, memories that were still fresh and raw. The teaching had been inconsistent with harsh rules and the punishments were often cruel. Would I be strong, kind, and gentle with enough backbone so the children will listen, learn, and enjoy school? Could I give children the joy of learning, the excitement as they read of worlds they knew nothing about? Arithmetic, that finally made sense and came together.

As I meditated on these questions and many more, my thoughts sauntered aimlessly back to the beginning where it all began. The traumatic events dragged me, figuratively speaking, to where I am today. I shivered as if a cold wind blew straight through my garments chilling me to the bone. The sun slid behind the clouds and I wrapped my arms tightly around my narrow waist. My thoughts floated around like snowflakes in a blizzard, wildly chasing memories and nightmares into fierce storms. My body shook, cold perspiration in droplets clung to my forehead, I gasped, forcing my breath to slow, taking deep even breaths.

The sun had peaked out behind the clouds, and the air began to radiate warmth and peace, I allowed my thoughts to go back past the pain and terror, and I was once again a little girl on my mother's lap. She was softly humming and hugging me in her rocking chair, her work-worn hands gently rubbing my back. The squeaks of the chair were pleasantly soothing. Her eyes were soft blue and they silently spoke of her love for me. Resting my cheeks on her breasts, my eyes fluttered, heavy with sleep. And that is where my story begins.

My name is Bella, my parents were Andrew and MaryJane Hunter and I was born in Philadelphia, Pennsylvania on June 14, 1860.

I don't remember much about my mother, she would rock and sing to me, rubbing my back and hair. She loved me and called me her little sugar plum. After Pa returned from the war, she gave birth to my baby brother, he was tiny, wrinkly and purplish. He never cried or even breathed. The angels took him away, leaving behind his fragile body. I examined his small fingers and toes, the tufts of hair clinging to his dainty head. His eyes were closed, his lips puckered, and he looked flawless just so small. Mother cradled him in her arms, tears of grief seeping down her face silently on his blue and white flannel blanket. I rubbed my fingers on her cheek, wiping the tears away. Pa cradled her head against his chest and she reached out and drew me close to them and we snuggled there for a lengthy time.

That evening as the dusky hues from sunset filtered through the narrow window, Mother started shivering uncontrollably. We wrapped her snuggly in quilts trying to warm her but she started sweating profusely and she tried peeling the quilts off of herself. She groaned as she rubbed her belly, her face tired and pale, her eyes glazed with fever.

Pa, his eyes filled with anxiety, gently wiped her face with a cool cloth trying to get her temperature down. The sheets were wet from perspiration, and as he folded the quilt back, his eyes widened in horror. My mother's lower half and the surrounding sheet were smeared with blood and varying sizes of clots.

"Get the doctor," Pa snapped as he rinsed his cloth in the pail of water already murky with the blood.

I fled, letting the door slam behind me, my bare feet pattering on the hard streets. The moon was far away in the night sky gazing down on me, the wind whispering 'run, run' in my ears. I ran until my chest ached, my breath coming in gasps. As I turned the final street corner, I saw the light flickering in the window, I was almost there. I gave one great burst of speed and reaching the door, I pounded and yelled desperately.

The door was opened by an older, portly gentleman. His eyes were gentle and he gazed in surprise at me, my hair a mess, face red and swollen from tears.

"Mother is sick," I croaked out and I slumped exhausted in a small, tired heap on the doorstep.

When I awakened, the sun was peeking over the horizon spreading its light through my window. The house was quiet except for noises of someone preparing coffee in the kitchen. I lay there resting still in a dreamlike state, when I remembered Mother.

Mother, how was she? I thought, scrambling out of bed leaving my covers, in a crumpled heap. I galloped down the stairs, my night dress swishing around my legs and into the warm kitchen.

Pa was sitting with his head in his hands at the table, exhaustion slumping his shoulders.

He looked up at me, his eyes dark rimmed and grief filled. He reached for me and I snuggled on his lap, his arms holding me close. He sipped from his coffee mug and I inhaled the rich smell of Pa's coffee and aftershave.

Pa took a deep ragged breath in, his voice full of pain told me that Mother had gone to be with Jesus. The angels carried her to heaven to be with my little brother. We sat there and cried for a while and then Pa asked me if I would like to see her. I nodded numbly and taking his large work worn hand we walked to the bedroom.

My mother was still and lifeless on the bed, body cold to the touch. There was no smile in her eyes as they were forever closed. No song on her lips, hands lay folded on her chest. She no longer would hug me close to her.

The pain from knowing that there would be no more hugs and kisses, singing as she cleaned and baked, made me weep. She was needed more here than in Heaven I thought bitterly to myself.

The next day she was laid to rest with my little brother tucked in her arms. The singers sang *Sweet by and by* as I lay wildflowers on her grave.

Pa and I turned and we walked slowly away to start a life without Mother.

Chapter 2

With Mother gone the house became silent. There wasn't much noise but the creaking of floorboards when someone walked across the floor or up the stairs. When Pa remembered to cook there was a banging of pots and pans and the sizzling noises of food cooking. Even those noises sounded listless and sad. He didn't hug and play with me like he used to, often he stared blankly at me as if he wondered what I was doing there. Occasionally, he came out of his trance-like state and reached for me, and I would cuddle next to him with my head on his chest. I would play with his ears running my fingers in the crevices rubbing my fingers along the earlobes, finding comfort and security being close to him.

When he did speak it was in a flat, barely audible tone. His blue eyes no longer sparkled with teasing and laughter. They were blank and the depths were like an ocean of grief. Even though my pa was physically present, I felt isolated, alone, in my world of pain. It seemed that I was invisible, that he no longer loved me. We just existed, our grief profound.

One day, I hurled the flower vase onto the floor, smashing it into many tiny pieces. I needed my pa to hold me, talk to me, love me! I needed his attention and his strength. I needed him back, the man with the joy and laughter.

A look of surprise flashed over his face but instantly it was gone. A veil fell over his features and I could not reach him. Pa reached for his brown medicine bottle and took a long gulp. He then wiped his lips with the back of his hand, sighing wearily, as he closed his eyes. He leaned back on his chair oblivious that I was there seeking his presence.

There were times when Pa's anger flashed for apparently no reason. He yelled and slapped me on the cheek, leaving a handprint that stung painfully. In a voice flat and hard, he said that he wished that I was the one who died. Occasionally, he used his old, weathered leather belt on me, if he had been drinking, he would beat me until my back and legs were full of stripes and blood trickled down my legs.

He would come into my room at night when I was in bed and sit on a chair hunched over, face in his hands staring at the worn floorboards. Most times he sat in silence, but I once saw him crying, tears leaking through his fingers, his shoulders heaving with sorrow. I laid there in the dark, silently watching him. When he finally lifted his head, I pretended to be asleep, not prepared to deal with this unpredictable man. He then slowly, stiffly rose to his feet and with an awkward pat on my head, left my bedroom. With eyes closed I listened to the floorboards as they groaned with the weight of his footsteps. I heard the click of his bedroom door as he retired for the night.

When Mother was alive the house would be filled with the rich aromas of baking bread, pastries and soups.

Whatever she made was delicious. I loved to eat the crust of fresh bread, still warm from the cookstove, smothered in butter.

Now, Pa often forgot about food but when he remembered, he would bring home cornmeal, beans, and salt pork. As time passed, he seemed more concerned with his brown bottle than with food.

One day when my stomach seemed to touch my back with hunger, I took a loaf of bread from the mercantile. A huge red-faced man grabbed me with his beefy hands, and shook me hard. My thin body trembled like a leaf and when I was released, I collapsed limply on the ground. He yelled that he never wanted to see my thieving face again. My head was spinning but I scrambled to my feet, stumbling in my haste to get away from him.

He reported my crime to Pa. Pa grabbed and hit me with his belt until I was covered in painful red welts. Screaming, I promised I would never steal again. His face was emotionless, his eyes vacant and distant. Finally, he threw down his belt and kicked me with his army boot and told me to leave and not come back for a long time.

My body was bruised and I was broken in spirit. Every movement was painful as I lurched to the door and down the steps. Leaning heavily on the railing to catch my breath, afraid that Pa would follow and finish what he started. Painfully putting one step in front of the other, I made my way to a small, rundown woodshed located in an abandoned lot, a few blocks from my house.

When I arrived, I doubled over, tears rushing like a river down my inflamed cheeks. Blood dripped through the back of my dress, my thin legs covered in painful red marks. I cried for a long time.

My senses picked up that I was not alone. With this feeling, my ears heard the sound of leaves crunching. I could hear someone or something stirring quietly. In my sadness I didn't raise my head, but sat motionless too afraid to move. Waiting, waiting, for what?

I could feel something soft and furry rubbing against my leg. Frozen with fear, my heart thudded rapidly in my chest. Slowly, cautiously I opened my eyes. On the ground near my knees, there was a skinny black and white animal with matted fur, so thin I could see her ribs. Deep inside this creature I heard a gentle rumbling noise like a little engine. To my surprise it was a beautiful baby kitten. I gently lifted her onto my lap, softly stroking her neck and back. The purring reassured me that she felt safe and I was able to calm myself. The two of us eventually dozed off.

My kitten and I were hungry, after searching, we found some bread the baker had thrown out. It was dry and had green spots on it. We devoured it and the hunger pains eased.

We hid for a long time, finally getting chilly. Eventually, careful not to be heard, crept back into the house.

The moon was round and orange that night the stars twinkled in the black night sky. I imagined that Mother and baby brother are looking down from heaven at me when the stars are bright.

The next day after Pa came home from work he brought me a new dress. I jumped up and down and clapped my hands. My dress was brown with yellow flowers and it had a wide skirt with lots of gathers at the waist. I twirled going around and around so fast my head felt spinny and my legs weak.

He had also brought home food. We had supper that evening.

The next day he hardly spoke a word. When he saw the kitten, he kicked it and it flew across the floor. She skittered away heading for the safety of the outdoors. Harshly, he told me to get the ugly varmint out. What is a varmint? My kitten is beautiful, it sounded like an ugly thing.

I found her hiding behind a tree in the backyard. Picking her gently, I carried her to the woodshed hoping she'll be safe.

That evening Pa smoked from his pipe. Swirls of smoke rose and curled above his dark hair. He drank from his brown bottle, and it seemed he was unaware of my presence. I left the house, closing the door softly behind me. The sun was going down and the rays of light colored the sky. I played in the woodshed with the fresh air lightening my mood.

My kitten had caught a fat mouse so she wasn't hungry. I used the wood shavings as plates and imagined having a huge meal, imagination doesn't take the hunger away.

I forgot to describe where we lived. Our house was tall and thin, the houses on either side of us are identical to ours. They are made of a dull red brick, with a porch on the front with a wooden bench swing by the door. I loved to swing on it with my doll.

Mother had made a cloth doll for me for my birthday. She has yellow yarn for hair which is combed into two braids, blue button eyes, and a red mouth. Her dress is blue gingham, like one I had when I was a baby. She wears a white apron with ruffles for trim. The shoes are made from black cloth and she is stuffed with old rags to make her soft.

There is a fireplace in the main room, with a wood box neatly stacked with chopped firewood and kindling. On the shelf above the fireplace was an ambrotype of my mother. She is looking away from the camera, her face serene and beautiful. Her hair was parted in the middle and combed neatly over her ears. The picture was taken the year before she married.

The table was across from it and covered in an off-white homespun fabric. It had neatly embroidered flowers and leaves on the edges of the tablecloth. Mother had made it years ago and had kept it in her hope chest. She had started to teach me embroidery, but my stitches were not very straight and even yet.

The settee is framed with dark wood and the fabric is a light beige. There are faded green leaves, orange and red blossoms randomly covering the seat and back. The fabric is rubbed thin in places with smudges on it.

The rocking chair has swirls etched on the back of the seat. Grandma brought it over from Scotland when my pa was a baby. The seat is smooth from years of rocking and soothing babies and young children.

The cooking area has a black cast iron cook stove, narrow cupboards and shelves on either wall. Blue gingham cotton fabric is pinned to the top of the cupboards to hide the contents on the shelves. They are now greyish with dust as no one has washed them now that Mother is gone. In the corner of the room are stairs that lead to the two small bedrooms upstairs.

In my bedroom there's a small crawl space in the wall where I play with my doll. I also hide there when Pa is angry or when I feel lonely and miss my mother. The bed is against the wall and is made from wood. The headboard and footboard are plain and of equal height. The straw filled mattress, lays on tightly woven rope frame. A quilt covers the mattress, it was made from fabric scraps Mother had saved through the years.

The days became shorter and frost covered the windows in the mornings. Snow had fallen a few times already and everything was covered in its chilly blanket.

Pa tired easily and would have a rest in the middle of the day. He blamed it on winter at first because of the lack of sunlight. His head would throb on a daily basis and he started to cough. One day after a particularly bad coughing spell, he noticed there was blood on his hankie. He ate very little and his clothes slowly began to hang loosely on him. He would drink from his bottle and claimed it made him feel better. I thought it made him sleep more during the day. As days and weeks passed, he wasn't getting better but only worse. When the new year arrived, he shivered with chills even when covered in quilts. He now coughed up a lot of blood when he coughed, which was often. Pa was too sick to get out of bed and lay thin and gaunt. The skin on his face clung to the bones, his eyes hollow and dark. He was a skeleton of the man who he used to be.

My mother's friend, Mrs. Barrett, stopped by occasionally with food. I enjoyed the visits as she often brought her daughter, Mary, along and I would have someone to play with. She also gave me hugs and cookies.

She made soup for Pa and would feed him with a spoon as he was too weak to feed himself. When she was not around, I fed him the leftovers that I heated up.

Mrs. Barrett showed me how to start a fire in the cookstove and how to test when the food was at the correct temperature. I listened intently and was cautious when I was cooking.

Sometimes my pa would cry when he talked about John getting killed, and the horrors of the war. He rambled about other things that I didn't understand and didn't make any sense. One day he was talking gibberish then he started moaning. Grabbing his quilts, he tore them off his bed.

"So hot." He sighed plaintively.

I stepped back and reached for a tin mug on the shelf. Quickly I filled it with water from the water pail. I handed him the lukewarm water splashing some on his hand. He struggled to sit up and stared at me with a glazed look in his blue eyes. I took a small step back. "Mary Jane?"

"No, it's me, Bella." I tried speaking calmly but my voice shook. Why was he acting like this? Why didn't he know me?

He slumped back down onto his bed.

"I'm sorry," he mumbled. "I have been a bad father. I love you, I'm sorry." The words were slurred and breathless. I leaned forward and strained my ears to hear his words.

He coughed a deep raspy cough. His hankie was stained with dark red blood. After the coughing spasm, Pa sighed and closed his eyes. He shivered and I pulled the quilt over his bony shoulders.

His breathing became shallower, slower, farther apart. He gasped a few times then was completely silent.

My breathing sounded loud in the deathly quiet room. The sounds of a mouse scurrying in the wall, the wind whistling around the house all seemed deafening in the stillness.

Eventually Pa's body grew cold and stiff to the touch.

I stood in the corner of the room and held my doll close. Finally, I slumped to the bare floor too weary to stand. I squatted awkwardly, the shadows in the room dancing eerily, the winter wind howling around the house making it shiver and groan.

As the darkness filled the room, I stiffly rose to my feet, legs sore from sitting too long in one position. Slowly, I walked across the room and gazed at my pa. His face was calm and relaxed. Cautiously I reached my hand to touch his cheek, it was lifeless.

I put my head on the bed, I had no one, my parents were dead and I was so alone. What was I to do? Who will love me? Who will take care of me? I sobbed my body shaking. I heaved deep gulps of air as the tears flowed. Finally, I slumped in complete exhaustion and slept.

Chapter 3

I slept poorly, tossing, and turning restlessly all night. My dreams were dark and menacing but I could not remember them when I awoke. My quilt lay in a tumbled heap on the floor and I shivered in the chilly room. Yawning, I stretched rubbing my swollen eyes, momentarily forgetting the pain of the previous night. When the memory returned, I slumped on my mattress in a heap, my arms hugging my legs, too emotionally exhausted to cry.

The warmth of the sun peeking in my bedroom window seemed to warm my spirit. I pulled the homemade curtain from the window and looking out realized that it was close to mid-morning. The wind had calmed during the night and the dark heavy clouds had lifted. The sky was now a clear blue, fluffy white cloud that floated in the distance. A scene of peace and serenity, a sharp contrast from the evening before.

I knew Pa was ill but he was supposed to get better. He was my only family left and I was too young to have no one. He had been a sullen, angry man, after he returned from the war, but I hoped things would return to what they used to be. I longed for my parents but now I was completely alone.

Tears rolled once again from my eyes, the world dark and lonely. The house was silent, no sounds of breakfast preparation or the strong smell of coffee being brewed. There was no one to hold me and tell me everything was going to be alright. My crying eventually subsided as I became numb to the pain.

I stiffly crawled off my bed, bending, I reached for the quilt on the floor. I heaved the heavy quilt onto the bed, straightened it and then tucked the corners in neatly, placing my cloth doll on the pillow.

Bleakly, I made my way downstairs into the kitchen. Finding bread, I took a sharp knife and tried sawing the loaf in slices. It didn't work well and ended up being messy lumps. I buttered it and slowly started to eat. Forlornly I chewed each bite and sighed deeply.

What should I do? I had no idea what should be done with a dead body? I knew that it had to be buried but I was much too small to dig such a deep hole. I placed my elbows on the table and rested my face in my hands. My hair was a tangled mess as no one had combed it in days. I slumped on the table and my mind went blank. I sat there quietly and after a while slivers of thoughts returned.

Thoughts of Mary, my best friend, her smile and giggle, her happy upbeat attitude. I mused on Mrs. Barrett's soups thick and rich with chunky vegetables and cubes of meat. It was as if I could smell her delicious cooking. Mary's brothers are lively and spirited and always teasing.

Mary is about five months older than I am. She has straight coffee bean colored hair and sparkling green eyes, she's chubbier than me and a lot of fun.

There are piles of children in Mary's family. She is in the middle with five older siblings, two sisters and three brothers. After her, there are 3 two-headed boys freckles sprayed over their snub noses. Most of the time they have dirt on their faces and grass and mud stains on their faded clothing. They enjoy teasing Mary and me, and I'm thankful they aren't my brothers.

The youngest is a tiny girl with soft curls in her golden-brown hair. Her name is Sarah and she loves to be held and gives slobbery wet kisses with her lips all pursed up. I played Peek-a-boo with her and held her. She's squirmy and wiggles a lot, I worry that she'll fall.

With my thoughts on Mary, I decided to go play with her, forgetting for a moment my grief.

I hadn't played with her for a long time because Pa was sick, although her mother had visited and brought food.

I pulled my cranberry knit hat from the wicker basket and the matching mittens. Mother had knit for me, the yarn coming from an old holey sweater of hers. I grabbed my faded grey, woolen coat, tugging it on, the buttons straining to stay in the buttonholes. My toes were squished in my boots and there was a small hole where my foot had worn through.

The sun was bright but the air was icy cold, my cheeks soon were frosty and snow clung to my eyelashes. Hurrying down the sidewalk, I was careful not to slip on the ice.

A carriage pulled by a dark chestnut brown horse pranced by me, its ebony tail flowing behind him. A blast of cold air hit my face as it sailed by. I gasped for breath in the frigid breeze, shivered, shoving my hands in my coat sleeves to keep them warm. A small child peered out of a passing carriage window, his nose flattened against the glass.

The streets were narrow and the snow had been shoveled off the sidewalks. Men strode purposefully, some stopping to buy a newspaper from a child standing on the street corners. The children called out that they had newspapers for sale, trying to earn a few pennies for food. They wore worn tattered clothing and looked cold on this chilly winter day. Other men went into the local hardware store, or headed to jobs or places of business.

Peering inside the hardware store, I saw men arguing heatedly over politics one man pounded the counter as he expressed his views on slavery. The nails on the counter clattered to the floor from his vehemence.

A couple of grey haired men intently played chess by the woodstove. The wood stove gave off a warm heat that I could feel from the doorway. Women chatted and exchanged news items with acquaintances. Others checked out the fabrics or bargained for a lower price on their groceries.

Finally, I turned away and started walking again. A thin calico cat dashed across my path, a small rat dangling from its mouth. A spotted black dog raced after it, swerving to avoid an oncoming horse, but slammed into his back leg. The horse reared, neighing in fear, his back leg kicked out grazing the dog on his side. The dog collapsed momentarily stunned on the ground, then fled in the opposite direction, forgetting the cat in his haste to get away.

The man in the carriage yelled some obscene words, and hit the frightened horse sharply on his back repeatedly. The whip was a long black snake whip, and I cringed at the sight of the cruel man beating his horse knowing how painful getting hit could be.

I plodded on for a few more blocks, the houses becoming smaller and more rundown. Mary's house was weathered and not much more than a shack. The paint was peeling from the dark green shutters, and the wind caused it to bang against the cracked kitchen window. The house with its peeling paint and broken porch step appeared tired and worn out.

Sarah's square white flannel diapers hung on ropes stretching across the alley, flapping stiffly in the freezing winter air. Beside them were pants in many shapes and sizes, patched neatly at the knees.

At Mary's, I knocked on the door with my cold stiff hand and entered when I heard a cheery "Come in."

Pushing the door hard, it opened with an irritating screech. Entering into the kitchen, I was met with the yeasty smell of rising dough, the smoky smell of the woodstove and the joyous laughter of happy children at play and work.

The wood stove had a small crackling blaze keeping the house toasty warm. A black kettle sat on the back whistling merrily.

Mary was finishing up the dishes and she hung her dishrag over the large cast iron washing pan. She grinned and I noticed she was missing a front tooth. She gave me a quick hug glancing at my red tear-streaked face but didn't mention it.

"Do you want to play with Sarah?" She suggested eagerly. "She's just learning to walk."

"Mary, can you get some tea, Bella looks chilled," Mrs. Barrett instructed briskly as she vigorously kneaded a large mound of bread dough. I watched as she worked, her cheeks rosy, sleeves rolled up to the elbows, arms plump and strong. Flour covered her checked cotton apron and a smear was across her cheek where she had brushed away a stray hair.

"My pa died," I blurted abruptly, starting to sniffle.

Mrs. Barrett quickly washed her hands in the dish water, drying them on a towel that lay on the cupboard. She wrapped her arms around me, and I rested my head on her ample bosom.

"Just let it out, dear child," she murmured as she wrapped a strand of hair around her finger curling it. Her hands cracked and reddened from years of hard work were gentle. I rubbed my face on her shoulder, drying my tears and runny nose on her faded brown dress.

Mary gave me a gentle smile and reached out, softly squeezed my hand. Turning she left to get the mugs for tea. The boys crowded around pushing, shoving, faces smudged with dinner. Their clothes were well worn but neatly mended.

Sarah crawled over to me, and lifted her arms and asked to be picked up. Mrs. Barrett lifted her and set her on my lap. I nestled my head into her shoulder, inhaling the sweet clean baby scent, feeling the soft curls against my cheeks. Wrapping my arms around her waist, I grinned down at her. Sarah placed both hands on each side of my face and looked earnestly into my eyes.

"Ba la," she lisped.

"Sarah said my name," I said in awe. The boys grinned and tickled her on her tummy. She giggled and squirmed until I had to put her down.

Mary returned with steaming mugs of tea. Inhaling deeply, I breathed in the minty fragrance, placing my hands around the cup my fingers tingle with the heat. After my tea was savored to the last drop, I stretched my feet towards the wood stove wiggling my toes, loving the way they felt in the heat.

Relaxing in the presence of my friends, the fire crackled in the woodstove. The atmosphere was calm and safe. Mrs. Barrett continued to massage my back using pressure with her broad palms, on my shoulder blades where it was tight. "We will take care of the funeral arrangements," she stated gently.

I nodded gratefully.

"Mary, why don't you and Bella play with the little children? I need to finish my baking." She sighed, suddenly appearing weary.

We spent the afternoon playing with Sarah. Stacking blocks of wood for her to knock down, combing her hair. She became fussy so Mary rocked her to sleep. When she fell asleep, she was put in a dresser drawer that was made into a bed.

We then wanted to play dolls but the boys snuck up behind us and pulled our hair, jumping on the mattress trying to bounce us off. Mary and I chased them around the house, the boys knocking a water pitcher to the floor crashing it into many pieces. When we caught the boys we sat on them and pulled their ears.

Mrs. Barrett, hearing the noise, rushed into the room, her face furrowed and a stern frown on her face. She told us to get off the boys 'this instant' and sent us outside to take the clothes off the line and fold it.

The boys, after cleaning up the broken pitcher, were sent outside to chop wood into kindling for the fireplace.

Later that day, the rest of the family came home for supper of stew and fresh bread. The house could barely hold the energy of the family, the visiting, laughing and arguing.

The girls worked at the linen factory in town but I didn't know where Mr. Barrett worked. Two of the older boys were fighting in the war.

After supper, one of the big boys and Mr. Barrett left to dig my pa's grave. Mrs. Barrett and the oldest girl left to prepare the body for the funeral.

The day of the funeral was cold and clear, the service was at home. Pa's body was laid in a crudely built pine box, looking stiff and unnatural. I quickly turned away not wanting to remember him looking like that.

The speaker spoke for what seemed like a long time and I fell asleep from exhaustion, my head on Mrs. Barrett's lap.

Pa was buried in the local cemetery, I shoveled a scoop of dirt onto his casket and the others softly sang *Amazing Grace*. The adults lingered chatting in hushed tones, slowly returning to the house.

The neighbors brought food, stews, pies, baked beans and many other tasty dishes. We ate after the funeral sitting at the table or wherever we found a place to sit. The ladies washed and cleaned up before leaving one by one.

Mrs. Barrett told me that she would love for me to live with them but it was impossible as they were poor, and their house was bursting at the seams with all the children.

The Barrett's arranged for me to go to another family who had a ten-year-old boy. This boy would tease me and would throw horse droppings on me. He has pulled my hair and pushed me down onto the street and then kicked me when I was down. A couple weeks ago he chased me with a stick and I slipped on ice when I was running away from him. My leg started to bleed and he laughed uproariously when I cried. He then proceeded to hit me with a stick. A gentleman had come alongside and grabbed him by the shoulders, shaking him, and vehemently asked him to stop and go home. He has avoided me since that incident. I did not want to live there, so I told that family that I was going to Mary's place, and that the Barretts had changed their minds about me staying there. I hid in the cubby hole in the wall in my room until they left. When the house was quiet I knew that I was completely and utterly alone.

Chapter 4

The nights after my pa's death were long, the house would creak and shadows flickered mysteriously on the walls and corners of the rooms. The dark became dreadful as it felt that unknown creatures lurked waiting for me. I became fearful and would cover my body, making sure everything was covered, that nothing could touch or torment me in the dark.

Some nights I would sleep on my pa's bed, wrapping myself in his quilts. Breathing the smell of him now slowly fading. Memories of past days flooded my mind, some joy and laughter, others of pain and loss. Eventually my body and mind would give in to exhaustion and I would sleep restlessly, waking often to night terrors.

First thing in the morning when I woke, I would start the fire in the kitchen stove. The coals were still orange and hot from when I banked them the previous evening. Blowing on them, I placed small pieces of kindling until they started burning. Then I would place larger pieces of wood on the fire. The slow warmth of the heat radiated through the small room and I felt calmer than I had been in the night.

I put a kettle on for my tea, noticing that the tea leaves were almost gone, barely covering the bottom of the container. The cupboards were also getting bare and I knew that soon there would be no food in the house. This morning I mixed cornmeal with water and fried it in the cast iron frying pan being careful not to burn myself.

There had been food in the house after the funeral but now the supplies were depleted. Soup, baked beans smothered in molasses and bacon and cornbread were now a thing of the past. Hunger pangs were a familiar feeling, drinking hot tea eased those pains.

One morning in late February, when the sun's rays were spreading its light in orange and red hues over the horizon, I decided to head for the woodshed that I had played in before Pa's passing. I brought my cloth doll that my mother made for me, wrapping her securely in a small baby blanket that had been intended for my baby brother. It was still chilly outside some days and I didn't want her to be cold. It wasn't far from my house and the weather was mild and I enjoyed the fresh air.

When I got there, I played house with my doll. She would cry and I would rock her and sing to her. She didn't really cry as she was a doll but I pretended to cry for her. She finally settled and I set up small pieces of wood chips for the plates and leaves for the teacups.

We were in the middle of a pretend supper when my cat strolled in looking agile and beautiful. When I saw her, I realized that I had really missed her. She rubbed her body against my legs winding around them, purring loudly. I lowered myself to the ground and I reached to pick her up and placed her on my lap. She started kneading her paws into my stomach, as if she was making bread and my stomach was the dough. I could feel her sharp claws digging into my skin and then releasing.

I smiled and scratched her head and rubbed my hands down her black furry back. "What should I call you?" I questioned thoughtfully as I gently stroked her.

"Purrr purrr," she replied.

"That's a good name," I decided, "You know how to say your own name, your name is Purr," and I grinned to myself.

I looked her over carefully. "You're getting chubby, you must be catching a lot of mice." I eyed her critically.

We spent a few more minutes together until Purr marched off with her tail high in the air. I called her back but she ignored me not even to turn around and look back.

While I was spending time with my cat, the air had turned bitter. Snow had begun to fall from the darkening skies. The wind blasted through the cracks in the woodshed and through my winter coat, chilling me to the bone. I began shivering from the cold, glancing through the doorway into the stormy evening.   Stretching, I picked up my doll and headed towards the street. The icy breeze whipped snow around me, blinding me at times as it descended furiously. The streets were damp and slippery, and I walked with care, slipping and sliding on the icy spots.

On the side of the road, not far from the woodshed, stood four large sheds. Coal oil was stored there in wooden cylinder barrels and were neatly stacked in tiers up to the ceiling of the buildings.

I wondered if I should stay there until the storm blew over. "No, I need to get home," I said to myself in the deepening shadows.

I ran as fast as I could, snow falling steadily around me. Storm clouds covered the sun and visibility was poor. I peered through the shadows for my house, my safety in this winter storm. My face was wet and cold, my hands felt like blocks of ice. Finally, I saw my home and I quickened my footsteps. Reaching the steps I tripped on a broken board, slushy from the damp snow and ice. I landed hard on my knees, my hands partially breaking the fall.

Tears filled my eyes as pain radiated from my knees and up my legs. I half crawled, half dragged myself inside the silent, cold house. My leg throbbed but I ignored it, there were more important things to focus on now. I hobbled over to the firewood box and grabbed some kindling for the fire.

I had been taught how to start a fire when I was younger. I had been warned to never play with fire and was shown how to be safe while making it. Pa explained that a fire could get out of control very quickly if not watched carefully. He had also shown how to bank the coals so the house will remain warm at night. I had watched him many times so I knew exactly how he did it.

Soon a small orange flame began to lick at the kindling. As the fire grew stronger, I placed another small log on the flames. The fire slowly warmed me and I rubbed my hands briskly together trying to get them to thaw. My body tingles from the heat, the flames danced cheerily caressing me with its warm presence. I could relax now that I was home and safe, protected from the freezing elements outside.

Now that task was taken care of, I peeled my winter layers of clothing off hanging them on chairs in front of the fire to dry. I then squatted on the floor to examine my leg. It had been bleeding so I wiped the excess blood off with my skirt. It started bleeding again, so I took a damp rag and held it on the wound until there was no more red seeping through the cloth.

My stomach growled hungrily and felt tight with pain. After scrounging in the kitchen cupboards for a while, I found a small piece of the last cornbread. It wasn't fresh and it was crunchy but I ate it and it took the stomachache away. I also had a cup of hot water.

It snowed heavily during the night and into the next day. The second evening it turned into rain and I listened to the gentle pattering as the drops hit the windows and roof.

I was in a deep dreamless sleep when I woke to the shrill, piercing shriek of the town fire alarm. At first I didn't know what the noise was. Disoriented, I rubbed the sleep from my eyes, stumbling to my bedroom window blearily peering through.

What I saw woke me from my sleepy stupor, bright red-orange flames danced dangerously in the distance, flames leaping, growing stronger as the breeze caught it up. Sparks shooting for the skies landing on rooftops, trees the ground.

Staring in horror, my eyes widened in shock. I needed to leave now and find a safer place away from the swiftly growing flames. I threw my blue flowered print dress over my nightgown and raced down the stairs, missed the last step and landed hard on my bottom, legs and arms splayed out wildly. Clumsily I got to my feet and grabbed my winter coat, stuffing my arms in the sleeves. Boots were shoved on my feet, mittens and hat were on.

Running back up the stairs, my boots making loud clunking noises as I pounded on the wooden boards, searching frantically for my doll, I bent down and looked under my bed. There was dust but she wasn't there. Where was she? Where could she be? What had I last done with her? I paused for a moment to reflect. Mother used to pray when she was in trouble so I bowed my head and folded my hands and prayed earnestly, yet quickly knowing that time was short.

"Dear Jesus, help me find my doll and keep me safe. Thank you. Amen."

Calmness came over me and I remembered that I had her in bed with me last night. I rummaged through my heap of quilts and found her crammed in between the wall and the bed covered by the pillow and quilts. I grinned as I pulled her from her hiding place and gave her a squeeze.

I tore down the stairs, careful not to trip on the steps, and I raced outside. The smoke billowed from the fire and the dark night skies were turning a murky grey. The twinkling stars were hidden from view.

The fire burned brightly in the direction of Blackburn & Co. petroleum sheds. 2000 plus barrels of refined oil were in flames. The burning oil flooded the streets and sewers destroying everything in its path, flames angrily, hissing and crackling as it grew in size and strength. Houses, schools, streets, nothing could stop its deadly force. Streets cracked from the intense heat.

I fled, eyes wide in terror, clutching my doll, the only possession I now had left. I shoved my way through the crowds of frantic people weaving around and under them using my small size to my advantage. I used all my speed and skill as I desperately tried to find a way to escape.

Struggling in the slush, I slipped and fell and rose again. The streets were filled with panic-stricken people trying to find safety, searching for loved ones.

My ears rang from hearing the screams of agony, pleading, begging for help. Their cries of terror and pain as those unable to get out of the raging inferno, slowly roasted to their death. The fire was their grave.

Families called in desperation to each other, children crying, fear was hovering like a cloud over the city, enabling me to run like I had never run before.

My heart pounded loudly in my chest and I gasped for air. The air was thick with coal smoke and I struggled for each breath. I wrapped my knitted scarf over my mouth and nose to keep out the strong odors. My bloodshot eyes burned painfully from the toxic fumes.

A panic-stricken mother cradling a small child on her hip, rushed over to me and grabbed my arm frantically. With a voice cracking with fear she asked if I had seen her little boy.

She unwittingly squeezed my arm painfully as her mind was focused solely on her missing child.

I shook my head mutely, as I hadn't seen him. She released her grip and tingles ran up my arm. Her sob filled calls faded in the distance as I continued my way to safety.

Behind me, firefighters fought the deadly oil spill. Rescuing people, saving lives. I could hear them as they called out to each other giving abrupt instructions, not wasting their breath on needless words. Courage and strength in the face of the vast destruction, gave me the strength to continue on.

My feet had wings and carried me away, far away. My boots were full of slush, feet and hands numb with the cold. My coat dripped with moisture from me falling repeatedly. I was chilled to the bone. I shivered, the icy breeze freezing me but finding strength, I courageously fought my way to safety.

My chest ached, my breath seemed to have been squeezed from my body and I gasped desperately for life, to breathe. My legs trembled in exhaustion and they felt as strong as jelly, unable to hold my weight any longer. Fire now appeared to be on the horizon but the choking smoke encompassed the city.

I slumped against a red brick wall of a department store. My legs had given out, too weak to hold my exhausted body, I slid to the ground in a crumpled heap, face smeared in soot. Trails ran down my cheeks where tears had cleared my face. I clutched my doll close, the only comfort I had in this frightening world.

Faces blackened from smoke huddled in groups, cheeks streaked with tears and eyes fearful. Babies and small children wailed, mothers speaking softly or quietly singing, soothed the children. Fear and anxiety in all hearts, but some with true courage, spoke words of encouragement helping where it was needed.

Slowly, the subdued colors of the sunrise spread across the devastation. The varied shades of pinks, blues and orange filled the horizon in glory. The sun's glow slowly warmed the earth and filled it with light, totally oblivious of the havoc of the terrifying night.

Lifting my weary head and bloodshot eyes, I noticed that the crowd was straggling towards a whitewashed church. Rising stiffly to my feet, my legs still feeling shaky, I cautiously followed at a safe distance.

Ladies were bustling around carrying serving dishes of steaming food. I breathed in inhaling the smells of cooking. The rich aromas teasing my nose, tantalizing and tempting me. I could smell fresh bread and I could almost taste the crunchy crust smothered in butter and the softness of the bread. I then realized I had no idea when I had last eaten, but I did know that I was hungry and my stomach began to growl.

As I cautiously stepped closer a lady who appeared to be friendly, waved me to come closer. She showed me where I could wash my face and hands and when I was cleaner she gave me a bowl of soup filled with vegetables. The soup was heavenly, full of goodness and tiny chunks of ham. I was also given a thick slice of bread and it was even better than I had imagined.

The nourishment filled me and with the warmth in my inner being, I became sleepy. I wandered inside the church and found a bench and I curled up on it. I wrapped my doll tightly l in my arms, and putting my thumb in my mouth I drifted to sleep. In my sleepy state I could feel a lady, removing my sodden winter coat, mittens and boots. Then tucking a warm, thick quilt around my shoulders she gently patted my back with a gentle smile on her motherly face.

My dreams were filled with my own mother who had rocked and sang to me. When I awoke, I was saddened since I could not remember her face.

The firefighters fought for hours. A few stopped by the church to eat and rest, their faces blackened from smoke and creased with fear and exhaustion. They then returned to fight the flames trying desperately to save lives andhomes.

Another batch of men would eat, rest and return to fight the flames. This continued all day and finally, just before nightfall, the last spark was extinguished.

The firefighters returned to the church building and ate silently. Their faces were drawn and full of complete exhaustion. From my bench where I was relaxing, I listened to the news of the devastation.

It was mentioned that three city blocks were completely destroyed and at least thirty people were killed in the flames. Some burned beyond recognition. They did not fully know the extent of the damage but they thought that it could be around a half a million dollars.

February 8, 1865, would be a day I wouldn't forget.

The weary men left, shoulders bowed as if they carried the weight of the world on their shoulders. It had been a very difficult day.

The next day, I worried about Mary, her home was located close to the fire. Was she safe? Where was she?

Almost a week later, I happened to meet Mary's sister. She was making her wayhome from work. She squeezed me tightly as if afraid to lose me. In a voice choked with grief, she informed me that her mother and Sarah had lost their lives in the flames. Her father and an older brother had been badly burnt while they were fighting in the fires. They were slowly recovering. The younger children had been sent to relatives across the country. Mary was now living with her uncle and aunt in Pittsburgh.

Upon hearing the sad news I plopped onto a nearby bench. I cried as if my heart was breaking. The loss was so great. How I had loved Mrs. Barrett and Sarah and I hoped that I could see Mary again. Mary's sister cried too.

Eventually, she slowly rose to her feet and quietly stated that she had to return to the boarding house before the curfew. I stood and tightly wrapped my arms around her, smelling the oil from the sewing machines and the cloth she worked with, all mixed together in a dusty smell. She gave me a quick squeeze and gave me a gentle kiss on the cheek. Her face was damp from tears, her eyes reddened and swollen.

"Take care of yourself," she said lovingly, her voice gruff with deep emotion. With a thoughtful pat on my tangled mess of hair she retreated into the long shadows of the evening. I sighed with the empty, lonely feeling that wanted to overwhelm me and with my head down I shuffled my way to the makeshift enclosure that was now my home.

It had previously been in a small building but now it was falling apart and it wasn't being used anymore. I had put up cardboard on the walls to keep the icy winter out. I also had stolen the quilt from the church and my doll that Mother made comforted me on my long cold nights when I tried to stay warm.

I turned to look up at the sky and the moon, looking like a man with a round orange face, gazed down on me. Predictable in its many phases, sending calmness to my tumultuous emotions.

Chapter 5

After the fire, life settled into a dreary drudgery. Dull aching hunger pangs stirredme awake in the morning and my first thought was always of food. At night the ache in my stomach kept me from sleeping, and when I finally fell into a fitful sleep my dreams were filled with raging fires and the screams of the dying. I would wake covered in a cold sweat, shaking with fear. I curled tightly in a ball, legs tucked into my chest, head resting onmy knees, my arms securely holding it all in.

When the light slowly and gently kissed the horizon, spreading sunbeams of light across the sky, I would unfold myself and rise to face the dawn of a new day. Every day wasthe same in its monotony. The first place I would stop was at the bakery, the workers would throw out the old baking when they opened in the morning. It was dried out or often had greenish spots on it. This morning I found a bit of pastry with sliced apple. That was a rare treat.

My next stop was the diner. There I sometimes found leftover food scraps orpotato peelings in the garbage. If I got lucky I would find a sliver of meat dried and moldy, but nourishing. I walked many blocks every day looking in the trash for food to feed my belly. Sometimes people would see me digging in the garbage and they would yell and try to chase me away. They once got the police after me but I was able to escape because I knew all the hiding places in the back alleys. After that I was more careful not to be seen and went out at dusk or when the stars and moon were out, for a while.

One night as I hunted for scraps of food, I surprised a raccoon and he attacked me. His teeth and claws were extremely sharp and left deep scratches on my arms. I had put my arms up to protect my face so my face was uninjured. Between the fear of meeting the wild animal and the burning pain of the scratches, I started to scream. My screaming scared the raccoon and he took off on his short stubby legs, disappearing quickly into the darkness.

Nearby I saw a lantern flicker on in a house. I suppressed my screams when I saw an older balding gentleman peer out of his doorway. The light behind him coming from the inside of the house cast shadows and he looked white and pale like a ghost. His face appeared hollow and his body was thin. The lantern's light made the shadows bounce like a crazy living thing. He held the lantern high, swaying it back and as he walked slowly, his unsteady footsteps sounding deafening in the quiet darkness. He looked intently into the shadows. I shrank behind a large shipping crate trying to take up as little space as possible. The light from the lantern flickered by me and I was not observed. It took a long time for my breathing and heart rate to return to normal.

My wounds bled for a while and I used the hem of my skirt to stop the blood flow. Holding my hand on top of the cloth and applying pressure the bleeding eventually subsided. I then wiped the excess blood from my arm and face.

April arrived slowly, first as daffodils with their sweet faces upturned toward the sun. The trees began to bud which eventually would be deep green leaves as a covering for the trees. Underneath last year's faded and tired grass the tiny new spikes slowly pushed its way upwards toward the light. The dreary winter had turned a page and everything was becoming new and fresh again.

Geese filled the skies in small groups as they returned from their warm winter homes.

They foraged on the fields looking for food. Some flew on to more northern locations while others stayed and built nests, laying eggs preparing for their future family.

One early morning, as the sun spread its warm rays over the horizon, church bells began to ring, their beautiful music echoing up and down the city streets through the alleys and the slums of the city. At first, I paid no attention as church bells always rang early on Sunday mornings. I came to the realization that today was not a Sunday as no one was dressed in their finest clothes and people were going about their daily lives.

People gathered in stores and street corners or curiously strolled out of their homes to investigate the reason for the bells ringing at such an unusual time. I too had become curious.

In the distance I heard shouting but could not make out the words. As the crowd grew nearer and began to gather on the streets I could then make out the joyous yells.

"General Lee has surrendered." The bloodiest war in history was over. So many lives lost, families torn apart. It is now over. Abraham Lincoln can bring this country healing and rebuilding after the huge losses.

The happy news was carried by the people until everyone knew that the war was over. The union had won. What an amazing day, the very air felt festive.

Someone started to dance and soon the streets were filled with dancing, laughing couples. A grey haired gentleman in a neat navy suit started playing a catchy tune on his fiddle.

Women's hoop skirts swirling wildly, their white lacy petticoats flashing as they spinned and twirled in the streets. There was a joyous abandon, rhythmic tapping of feet, to the music on the hard streets, laughter; merry and light.

Men blew horns in the celebration, others shook bells. The joy was tangible; it was real and alive. Hats were thrown in the air with loud hoorays, singing echoed throughout the streets. No one cared if you sang on tune or not.

Women and children ran freely carefree, through the streets waving ribbons of red, white and blue. They wore the patriotic colors in their hair in bows or tied at the end of braids. Flags flew proudly in the celebration. The Civil War was over! It was finally over!

My pa had fought in the war against the Confederates until he had been injured and sent home. He had told me once that all men should live free and he believed that it was wrong to own another person.

"We are all equal in the eyes of God," he had said, his blue eyes were serious. He'd be pleased that the war was over and the slaves were free. He had suffered so much because of the war. The memories had been so hard on him.

He had wanted to forget the bloody war but it couldn't shake him. He was a completely changed man after he experienced the horrors of war.

Thoughts on Pa made me lonely, tears spilled freely from my eyes and dripped down my dirty face. My nose dripped and I rubbed my nose against my filthy sleeve. I missed my mother and him so desperately. There was an ache in my heart that felt like physical pain. Knowing that I would never see them again was too hard for me to comprehend fully. I sat there with my back leaning against the brick building. My shoulders slumped and my head resting wearily on my knees. As I watched the parties and their gaiety, all I felt was profound sadness and loss.

The early spring air was still chilly and I wrapped my arms around myself trying to keep warm. I sat there for a long time thinking of my family. As the sun rose in the sky, it warmed me and I became sleepy and dozed off for a few moments.

My hunger pangs woke me and I stretched, rubbing my eyes red and swollen from the tears. My face was streaked but I was oblivious of how I looked. My focus was on finding food, the hunger making me feel weak and shaky.

Since there was so much distraction from the news, finding food would be easier I thought, my instincts were correct.

When the plump white-haired grocer was slicing meat for a customer I grabbed a loaf of freshly baked bread. I tried to appear nonchalant as I slinked towards the door, I was small and it was easy for me to escape with all the people there.

The mercantile was crammed with folks out to celebrate the end of the war.

There were grizzled farm hands in desperate need of a shave and bath, smelling of cows, tobacco and unwashed bodies. They were slouching against the counter chewing tobacco spitting on the floor or between people's feet.

Fine ladies in beautiful flouncy dresses in appealing shades of many colors and fabrics. Their button up shoes tapped as they delicately walked on the worn plank floor.

Soft soothing ladies voices clear and sweet making pleasant small talk. Deep strong tones from the men rumbling as they discussed and argued over politics. High pitched shrieks from children, intermingled with bursts of giggling, as they played outside. The noises filled the room and spilled out of the doors.

A grey haired pair of suspendered men sat on stools in front of a chess game on the porch. One thoughtfully chewed on a straw as he pondered his next move. The other pushed up his round eyeglasses and whistled nonchalantly off key as he waited for his opponent to take his turn.

I was unnoticed in the bedlam and was able to sneak away in safety.

I enjoyed a small chunk of bread and saved the rest in a safe place for later.

Chapter 6

The next few days were rainy and fog covered the ground in the morning. One night there was a thunderstorm and I cowered in my shelter trembling in fear from the lightning flashes that lit up the night skies. The deep rolling thunder felt too close for comfort. I prayed that it would pass quickly. Eventually the rumbling eased and the flashes of lightning faded into the distance until it ceased all together. I was then able to fall into a restless sleep.

On April 15, 1865, bells tolled throughout the city of Philadelphia. The rhythms were deep and melancholy, sounding as of suffering. This time it was for loss, an unthinkable suffering too dark for me to fully grasp at my young age. Flags were flown half-mast, houses had black ribbons hanging from the doors and windows indicating a death.

People soberly mingled on the streets speaking in subdued tones, an atmosphere of sadness was heavy as a deep grey fog on a starless night, waiting and ready to suffocate us in its gloom.

The nation was in mourning.

The news brought the horrifying information that our president Mr. Lincoln was assassinated. He was holding his wife's hand as he watched a play in the local theatre. He was shot in the back of the head.

The assassin had yelled 'Sic semper tyrannis' (thus always to tyrants.) He then leaped out of the theatre booth breaking his leg, but was able to escape capture from the security guards. He then disappeared riding on a horse.

President Abraham Lincoln passed away from his injuries the following morning. He was cared for at a locally owned boarding house, the Peterson's, surrounded by those who knew and loved him.

The War Department quickly put up a $100,000 reward for the capture of John Wilkes Booth. There was now a massive nationwide manhunt for the killer. He first fled to Maryland where there were confederate sympathizers and he hid in the woods there. Twelve days later he was tracked to a barn in rural Northern Virginia. His companion David Herold surrendered almost immediately but John Wilkes Booth fought for his freedom.

When he refused to exit the barn, the authorities lit a fire with the intention of burning him out. When the flames became unbearably hot, the barn began to give way as the fire began to burn through the beams. Smoke billowed in a suffocating cloud as he attempted his escape.

He was shot immediately in the neck and fell in a crumpled heap on the ground. He was paralyzed from the neck down and pleaded with the authorities to take his life, which they refused. Several hours later, he succumbed to his injuries.

Meanwhile his co-conspirators had been captured. They got varying punishments from death to prison sentences depending on the severity of their involvement with the crime.

The original plan was to kidnap Abraham Lincoln but that turned out unsuccessful so they changed their plans to assassination.

The news made me sad, knowing that this was a monumental time for our country. We had just gone through war and we needed healing and rebuilding from our grievous losses. I didn't fully understand all the politics of Mr. Lincoln's murder but I heard so much information about the tragedy. It gave me things to ponder as I walked about the town searching for food and in the darkness of the night when I am alone with my thoughts.

Not everyone was sorrowful. I overheard two gentlemen in fine suit coats having a passionate discussion on the street as I walked past, my head bowed so they couldn't see my unkempt hair and clothes. The younger man was speaking loudly to the older one and was saying, "That Abe Lincoln deserved what he got. Someone should have killed him sooner. He was just a slave lover."

The men moved on out of my hearing but I thought about it all day. Those beliefs were different from those of my parents. What was wrong with loving slaves, were they not people too?

As I pondered the subject, I wondered if those with slaves would lose money if they had no one to work their fields? This would affect their lifestyle and many other areas in their lives.

I could then understand why the men had said that because it was awful being poor. I remembered the days when food was set on the table and our family would sit around, and Mother and Pa would discuss their day. I really missed those times of peace and family. The memories were getting harder to recall. When the memories didn't return, I recalled the feeling, it felt warm and cozy like a soft, thick blanket on a cold night. The feeling of love and safety when it seemed nothing could hurt our family.

I shook myself gently to get myself back to reality. I was hungry. The sun setting on the horizon colored the skies in orange and pink hues, the shadows were lengthening making familiar things dark and menacing. It was harder to find food in the dark, feral cats, dogs, raccoons, maybe a skunk or two would start hunting in the shadows of the night. After my encounter with the racoon I had no interest in it happening ever again.

Mr. Lincoln's body was delivered to its final resting place in Springfield Illinois, his hometown, by train. His son Robert Todd Lincoln was with him and they also brought Abe Lincoln's son, Willie who had passed three years previously. His wife Mary Todd Lincoln chose to stay in Washington DC as she was too upset with her husband's passing to emotionally withstand the trip. The train came through over a week after his passing.

The streets were packed with people that day, it seemed everyone wanted to have one last glimpse of our beloved president. The crowd surged towards the train station and I got swallowed up by the crowds of people. I kicked, hit and struggled but it was fruitless, I was just too small and the crowd was so large. Defeated, I accepted that I was going to see Mr. Lincoln in his coffin.

I did not want to see another dead person. I had experienced too much death and I felt worn out and sad with all the death. Dead people looked scary to me, all stiff and their faces an unnatural color. I would have bad dreams after seeing them and sometimes the dreams would be recurring, and I hated that. Waking up in fear with all the dead faces in my dreams, shaking in fear covered in a cold sweat. Unable to sleep for the rest of the night.

The line was long and my legs were becoming shaky from standing so long. I wanted to sit but the crowd didn't allow that as everyone was packed so tightly. I sighed wearily to myself. I wanted out.

Many fought their way into the line, desperate for one last final goodbye. Tempers flew as people shoved and pushed their way trying to get to the head of the line. Clothing was ripped, and a lady had her arm broken when she stumbled, the crowd knocked her over and stepped on her.

Wailing, silent tears, anger, denial, and heartbreaking acceptance at Mr. Lincoln's premature death were the emotions of the 300,000 people who showed up to say their final farewells.

Mr. Lincoln was tall and thin, face gaunt and lined but he looked at peace. The demands of the war had aged him beyond his years. His grey eyes, once full of compassion, were deep set and closed forever. His nose was sturdy, with extra-large ears, hair was full and black with grey strands woven among the dark ones, his hair was neatly combed. The beard covered his chin and hollow cheeks. Strong hands folded on his chest were rough from years of manual labor. His features were still as he lay stiff and silent in his coffin.

I was relieved when the crowd released me from its clingy grasp and I was able to escape. My stomach churned from the smell of death and enclosed within the group for so long.

Seeing the dead body brought back painful memories that I didn't want to think about. Memories that I tried to repress and put in the back of my mind. They came back in a raging flood and I sobbed brokenly from the loss of my dear parents, and my little baby brother whom I never got to know. I fell asleep that night in my shack, my face streaked with tears curled in a tight ball, an orphan all alone in the world.

The next day, at the crack of dawn, Mr. Lincolns' funeral train left Philadelphia and continued through the nation to Springfield, Illinois which was his hometown. This would be his final resting place. His beloved son Willie was buried beside him. His burial was May 4, 1865, at Oak Ridge Cemetery in Springfield.

Chapter 7

Life continued its endless bleak march forward. Nights were spent hiding in the cold makeshift shelter, trying to keep warm, the spring nights were still a bit chilly. The quilt that I had stolen from the church kept me cozy, it was worn, seams coming undone being outside constantly had worn it out prematurely. My doll was tucked snuggly in the folds of fabric, when I was not around.

I am careful not to be observed but nobody seems to notice a bedraggled dirty little girl. I leave them alone as they do me.

The days slowly grew warmer as spring turned into summer. I went barefoot as my boots had finally fallen apart, too damaged to be repaired. I wiggled my toes in the dirt enjoying the feeling as it slipped between my toes. The warmth of the sun felt good as I wandered through the streets, in my never-ending hunt for food.

One day as I plodded past a mercantile I glanced into the window. There was a pathetically scrawny girl with thick matted blonde hair looking out at me, her eyes rimmed with dark lashes were large and blue in her thin face. Her cheeks were streaked with dirt and blood. The too tight dress was a muddy brown with small yellow flowers, it was ripped in several places and hung limply with dried mud, and blood on the skirt and blouse. It also had grass stains by the knees. Her feet were bare and stained black from going barefoot.

I stared in pity at this forlorn little waif. In horror, I realized that I was looking at myself. Revolting in disgust, I needed to clean myself up but how?

I had to figure out a way to clean myself up and get into clean clothes. Walking with purpose, I heard a bird whistling a cheery song and pausing to listen, I glanced around to check my surroundings. Around me were large family homes with clean crisp laundry flapping in the brisk breeze.

On one of the clotheslines hung a beautiful blue and white gingham dress. It had tiny pleats around the neckline and the waist. The sleeves were short with elastic and blue ribbon tied at the elbows. The length appeared to be about mid-calf. Beside them was a pair of bright white bloomers with a blue ribbon tied by the knee as trim. They appeared to be my size and relatively new.

Furtively I peered around me. There was no one around as far as I could see. I peeked in the windows, no one was in the main floor rooms. The house was quiet and still.

Cautiously I snuck to the clothesline. Reaching, I grabbed the clothing items, with a quick hard tug they flew off the clothesline. Fearfully, I fled, repeatedly glancing over my shoulder to see if I was being followed. No one seemed to pay any attention to me.

I found a tin rainwater bucket used to water garden vegetables in someone's backyard. It was full of murky grey water. I put the location into my memory, I would return after dark.

Today was a successful day for finding food. I found a slice of bread that wasn't too hard and potato peels, an apple was a delicious treat and the brown spot wasn't that big.

That evening when it was dark except for the stars and the little sliver of a moon, I found the water pail. When I was sure no one was around I stuck my hair in the bucket and scrubbed until it was clean. I then took off my clothes and scrubbed my face and body until the dirt was gone, shivering in the cold.

I quickly dressed in my new outfit. They were big but I loved them. I ran my fingers through my hair, like a comb trying to remove the tangles. After throwing my old clothes in the leafy shrubs I headed back to sleep.

I lived this way until it became cooler in the evenings. The trees gradually changed to vibrant shades of red, orange and yellows, evergreens contrasted with their dark rich greens. Days became shorter and cooler, children headed back to school.

I was sad since I wanted to be in school. I had attended for a few months last school term before my pa passed away. I knew my letters and could do simple arithmetic, I could sound out words on the advertisements on store windows. I desperately wanted to read, write and do sums.

The nights had a chill in the air. Frost appeared on windows in the early morning hours but disappeared when the sun rose in the clear blue sky. I shivered, tugging my coat around me in an attempt to warm myself. My wrists hung below my fraying coat sleeves and the faded grey shoes I wore were tattered and beyond repair. The buttons had fallen off and the soles flapped as I walked. The dress that I had stolen had large dark mud stains on the skirt. There was a long-jagged rip at the hem and a piece of skirt dragged on the ground from it hooking on a fence surrounding someone's yard.

The autumn wind blew the dying leaves off the trees, they danced merrily as they fluttered to their winter bed on the ground. When the last leaf was off, the trees stood bare and naked their leaf covering scattered around their roots. The once perky flowers wilted and fell from the once sturdy stems.

Geese headed south honking as they flew in their v shapes across the skies. They stopped in the fields, their baby goslings grown. They swam in the lake and ate the grain that remained in the field.

It wasn't long after, the first gentle snow fell from cloudy grey skies. The days turned desperately cold. One morning, the snow came up to my ankles. My feet were tingly with cold, then they went numb.

Finding food became a huge challenge, I dug through garbage cans hoping to find some pieces of food scraps. The hunger was constant, aching making me weak and dizzy. I was so tired I wanted to lay in the snow and sleep forever, my feet half frozen from not having boots.

Every day, I would go and painstakingly look for something to eat.

As winter progressed I was so weak that I could only crawl my rib's show my thinness, my stomach was round and protruding. My bones ached and I would rest for long periods of time trying to quell the dizziness that swirled in my head. A dull pulsating throb started in my forehead. It radiated over my head. My eyes blurred and I would have bright flashes of light with the pain.

I tried to ignore the agony in my search for food. I curled up in a crumpled heap trying to keep warm, rubbing my cold feet with my red chapped hands in an effort to stimulate blood flow. Slowly circulation came back.

I was behind a tavern hoping the cook would take pity on the stray dogs and feral cats that hunted in the streets. She often gave them leftovers from off the patron's plates. My stomach is cramping, from the lack of food. My body shivered violently, the bitter breeze swirling around the tavern, driving straight into my bones.

My head felt as if it would explode, a harsh cough from deep inside my chest shook me, I hacked up green phlegm tinged with red. Dry heaves made my frail frame shudder until I collapsed helpless and exhausted in the snow. My body shook with chills and then burned in fever.

I ripped off my coat feeling as if I was on fire. I threw it off leaving it in a tattered heap in the snow. I stumbled off down the road trying to get away from the burning heat trying to cool myself down. I did not know where I was going but something made me go. Then suddenly the heat was gone and I felt the intensity of the cold. The wind howled around me making my body like ice, but my coat was gone. I did not know where I had left it. I was lost. My head throbbed, and when I coughed my lungs felt as if they were going to explode. I shook with chills and then burned with a raging fever. I swayed as dizziness hit me and I stumbled and my bare feet slipped on the ice. My arms flailed wildly, helpless to break my fall. When I hit the hard cold ground, I knew nomore.

I felt a sense of peace as I lay in the snow, the cold and pain were gone and in the distance, a brilliant light shone. I felt myself rise and I moved in the direction of the radiant, glorious light.

Before me was a lush green meadow, fragrant flowers bloomed in magnificent beauty. Their sweet aroma perfumed the air and I inhaled deeply, the smell pleasantly calmed my senses. A bubbling brook trickled its way through the valley murmuring and splashing as it flowed. The breeze whispered and teased the leaves making them flutter gently, harmoniously.

In the distance, a sweet melodious voice sang clearly, beautifully in praise and worship. As I searched for the singers, I saw my beloved mother. She was holding my brother and was caressing his tiny soft cheek, her face glowed with pure joy. She looked carefree and her wavy chestnut hair framed her beautiful face. My brother kicked his feet, giggling and cooing, waving his hands joyfully in the air.

My handsome pa strode beside them and gazed tenderly down at my mother and brother. His face was now peaceful, the trauma from the war completely erased. The careworn look was gone and he was smiling.

They lifted their voices in thanksgiving to their redeemer.

"Mother, Mother I'm coming, wait for me," I cried, tears flowing down my face. Trying to run, my legs would not cooperate. They were so heavy, dragging me down.

The peaceful scene was shattered, I heard someone, the voice breaking through to my subconscious. Speaking in low hushed tones, gently pulling, forcing me away from my family. Compelling me to live.

I reached out for my family but they had turned and were strolling away. They had not noticed me. Pa's hand was on my mother's back and she gazed adoringly up at him. Pa's voice harmonized with her as they sang, their voices were heavenly, I had never heard anything so angelic.

They disappeared from my view and were gone.

"Mother, don't leave me," I shrieked hysterically, my heart breaking. Tears soaking my face in my pain.

"There, there," a soft voice crooned, her soft gentle hand stroking my hair.

"Here, have some broth, it will make you strong again. We didn't think you would make it. You are a very strong girl."

Her hand wiping the tears from my cheeks.

I turned my head to look at her, the voice came from a tall thin woman in a brown gingham dress. She was standing by the bed, her hair severely pulled back into a bun, nose long and thin. Grey eyes under thick brows were kind, lines around her eyes were smiling lines. Her mouth though wide, appeared gentle.

"I want my mother." I hiccupped sadly, shoving the mug away the contents splashing onto the quilt. Gasping for breath I fell back onto the deep, soft feather bed. A quilt with bright shades of blue, green and yellow was tucked securely around me.

"Where am I?" I croaked my voice rough and raw from my emotions and illness.

"My name is Emma and my brother Frank found you lying near to death, half frozen on the street. He carried you in," the woman stated her voice kindly. She had a loving, motherly voice.

"Please, take a sip of some chicken broth, you need to build up your strength."

Obediently I drank a few sips of the warm chicken broth and with a stifled sob snuggled under the covers. Miss Emma gently brushed my hair from my face. Leaning down she softly placed a kiss on my hair. Almost immediately I fell into a deep dreamless sleep.

Later from the depths of my subconscious, I heard a deep voice speaking with Miss Emma. Cautiously, I opened my eyes and saw a stout man with a mass of reddish grey curls. When he noticed that I was awake, he grinnedmerrily.

"You are looking better lass." His green eyes twinkled joyfully. He took out aninstrument from his black bag and put it on my chest and listened carefully. He did the same thing on my back, and then shook his headslightly.

"There's a bit of fluid in her lungs," he stated. "Keep giving her as much soup and liquids as you can and let her rest. Continue to put hot onion poultice on her chest in the evenings, it will help loosen things up in her chest. Prop her head with pillows, the wee lass is weak because of her rundown condition, and we don't want her to get pneumonia. It's a miracle she made it, she could still get worse." He stated somberly.

Turning, he placed a bottle on the stand beside the bed. "Give four times a day for seven days," he said gazing at Emma while running his work-worn hand through his hair making his reddish curls stand on end. Speaking softly he said, "You have done an excellent job." He then sighed and turned away from the bed. Miss Emma blushed slightly and nodded. "Thank you, I did my best."

Miss Emma gave me a spoonful of the medication, it made me sleepy and I then dozed off. When I awoke, the doctor was gone.

My strength took a long time to return. The healthy meals put color on my cheeks and I slowly gained weight. Weeks later I was allowed to walk around the house and eventually helped with light household duties.

After I had fully recovered from my illness, Miss Emma called me aside. With a look of sorrow in her eyes, she explained that as a single lady she was unable to permanently care for me.

"There is an orphanage in Gettysburg Pennsylvania." She continued, "The matron of this home is Mrs. Humiston." She paused momentarily to sip tea from her flowered teacup, and then continued with the story.

"Her husband, Amos Humiston, was found dead clutching an ambrotype of his three children in his hands. He was killed in the Battle of Gettysburg. This orphanage was opened for the soldiers' orphaned children.

"Dr. Bourns is in charge of the place and he takes care of the finances. They charge $25 a year for every child and that covers food and clothing. My church's Sunday School has agreed to support you financially so you can have a safe place to live."

$25 was a lot of money! How could the Sunday school ever afford the fees?

Miss Emma reassured me that I didn't need to worry about that. The money the children brought for their Sunday School collection would be enough to cover the expenses.

As I listened, emotions ran rampant through me. I was very grateful I wouldn't be living on the streets. I wouldn't be cold and hungry, I would have clean clothes to wear, not the rags I wore now. The best thing of all was going to school, I was very excited about that. I couldn't wait to learn my letters and do sums.

Although I was happy, I was still worried about the unknown. Sad, since I would be losing Miss Emma, I had grown to love and care for her deeply. I knew that I would miss her terribly.

My life was taking another twist. It appeared to be positive but I did not know what was around the next bend in my life but I prayed that I would be safe and have enough to eat.

Chapter 8

The following Monday, we left on our trip to the Orphans Homestead in Gettysburg. We rode in a dark brown carriage pulled by a pair of horses. One was a white horse with black speckles on his neck and back, the other was a solid grey with a white star on his forehead. I cautiously gave them each a crisp carrot and scratched their necks. I combed their manes with my fingers as I told them where we would be travelling today.

Mr. Frank hoisted me up into the carriage also giving Miss Emma a hand to help her up. He then energetically leaped into the drivers' seat snapping the reins and hollering, "Giddy up!"

He leaned back on his seat and started whistling "O Susanna" with gusto. The sky was a clear blue and the sun shone warmly as if to bless our travels.

Miss Emma and I sat inside the carriage, large windows on either side, so we could look out and watch the passing scenery. The bench which we sat on was hard, so Miss Emma had placed an old quilt on it to soften it.

Miss Emma had given me schoolwork when I was recovering from my illness and I worked on my sums to pass the time.

The ride was long and exhausting; the road was full of potholes. We bounced when we hit them, Miss Emma hit the roof on one deep rut, I let out a tiny chuckle and then quickly covered my mouth. I did not want to hurt Miss Emma's feelings. She saw me struggling to hold back my laughter and she started to giggle. We laughed until tears came in our eyes and ran down our cheeks. It felt so good to laugh. Mr. Frank turned around with a puzzled expression, I think that he is wondering if we lost our minds.

In places it was muddy and the horses strained their bulging muscles, to keep us from getting stuck. I called encouragement to them from where I was sitting. At one point, Frank had to get out and help them out a bit. We got out too so it wasn't so heavy for the horses to pull.

It would take us two long weary days to get to Gettysburg. We stopped in a small rundown tavern for a meal and the first night. The building was weathered and looked like it had seen a lot of years but the food was hot and flavorful, it was so good. I had never gone out for a meal before so I watched Mr. Frank and Miss Emma carefully with what table utensils they used and their table manners. I didn't want to embarrass them with my lack of knowledge.

We enjoyed finely sliced tender roast beef, with a heaping pile of creamy mashed potatoes smothered in rich gravy. There was fresh, buttered green beans on the side. For dessert there was a bowl of creamy rice pudding. I ate until my stomach ached with fullness.

After supper we relaxed at the table for a while. Mr. Frank and Miss Emma discussed the day and other small talk while sipping their coffee. I grew sleepy after a long day of travelling and a full belly of food.

Finally, they noticed that I was nodding off at the table, and they quickly finished their drinks. Mr. Frank picked me up and carried me to the room Miss Emma and I shared. I laid my head on his shoulder imagining that he was Pa. I breathed deeply and evenly so he would think that I was still sleeping.

The room had two cots and the mattresses sagged slightly in the middle. The beds were not as comfortable as Miss Emma's because they were made from straw and not as soft as her featherbed. I got into the bed and rolled into the middle doing that until I was exhausted from giggling.

There was an earthenware brown mottled pitcher and basin on a stand in one of the corners of the room. The basin was deep, with a soap dish attached. The soap had a flowery smell that brought back faint memory wisps of my mother.

Miss Emma had supplied me with a pair of bloomers, a petticoat, school dress, church dress and a flannel nightgown. She also provided shoes, stockings and a comb.

I put on my warm flannel nightgown. It was a pale pink with small red flowers. The nightgown had long sleeves with elastic on the bottom to make a ruffle. The neckline was high up to my chin. The skirt was billowy and went to my ankles keeping me warm at night. I loved it.

I then folded my underclothes and my dress neatly and placed them on a dark high-backed wooden chair. Pulling back the covers of the bed, I jumped in, snuggling under the quilt and tucking it securely around my shoulders.

As I drifted off to sleep Miss Emma quietly entered the room standing by my bed. She gently brushed my hair out of my eyes. Stooping, she softly placed a kiss on my cheek. The next thing I knew I was waking up to the smell of coffee brewing and the smells of breakfast being prepared. A rooster was crowing in the distance, another day had begun.

Breakfast was crispy bacon, easy over egg and fried potatoes with onions. I had homemade apple juice with my meal. Made from the apple trees that grew in the area. The adults had steaming mugs of rich black coffee.

We left as the sun was peeking over the distant hills, a misty fog encompassing us as we headed down the hard packed dirt road. The horses, fresh from their rest during the night, tossed their manes and trotted forward eagerly. As the sun rose on the horizon the fog lifted and we could see the green crops in fields. Trees with their new leaves stood proudly by the road and were scattered over the countryside. The signs of spring were everywhere as birds trilled and watched us from their nests. A deer and her fawn bounded fearfully away through the fields as we approached. Their white tails waving in warning.

I relaxed against the worn wooden bench, my feet tucked under me. I straightened my skirt covering my shoes and smoothing out the wrinkles. Miss Emma had given me a worn McGuffey reader to read, when I was comfortable, started to painstakingly sound out the words. I did not know how to read well but loved learning the stories in the book.

We arrived at the orphanage as the stars twinkled in the evening sky. The moon glowing in the distance, was a crescent shape.

I was slumped on the bench, deep into a dream when the horses stopped. The crisp spring evening air smelled fresh as Mr. Frank lifted me from the carriage. Miss Emma held my hand tightly as we walked towards the large whitewashed house, the house was dark except for a flickering light at the front of the building.

A plump dark-haired lady met us at the door. She introduced herself as Mrs. Humiston. There was a pile of paperwork that needed to be done after informing Mrs. Humiston of my parent's names. She wrote Andrew and MaryJane Hunter on a paper. I told her my birthday was June 14,1860. I could write my own name and neatly wrote Bella Hunter. After the signing and information was documented, we said our goodbyes. They wanted to rent rooms in the local town of Gettysburg for the night and needed to be on their way.

Miss Emma hugged me tightly and we both cried.

"I'll miss you, I don't want to stay here." I wailed, tears spilling from my eyes.

"I'm sorry, I wish it could be different," Miss Emma said, her voice sounding pained. She blew her nose discreetly into an embroidered handkerchief, her eyes were red and face blotchy. She gave one last desperate squeeze and they hurried out the door. Miss Emma turned for a long last gaze. A sob erupted from her as she quietly closed the door.

"We need to get you bathed, and wash your hair," Mrs. Humiston said briskly. "Can't have you bringing in fleas and other bugs."

She took my hand and quickly marched me to a room where there was a large tin tub. I thought that it looked like a horse trough but was too exhausted to comment on it. On a wooden chair there was a towel folded neatly and a bar of soap.

She unbraided and brushed my hair. From a shelf on the wall she reached for a small container. She squirted a coin sized amount of the solution onto my hair and rubbing vigorously made sure it completely saturated my scalp. My head felt like it was on fire, my eyes burned and I started to struggle, kicking, yelling and screaming.

"Take it easy child," Mrs. Humiston said calmly. "I'm using kerosene to kill the fleas and bugs."

I tried to calm myself but my chest heaved with sobs. She proceeded to rinse my hair using a small container with water as I leaned over the tub. Using a fine tooth comb, she carefully went through my hair. When she was sure there were no fleas remaining, she took a pair of scissors and cut my hair shoulder length.

Removing my clothes, I climbed into the tub filled with warm water. Mrs. Humiston washed me with a nasty smelling lye soap. When I was all pink from the water and scrubbed clean, she dried me off with a faded brown towel. My body felt fresh and tingled from the soap. My eyes burned from the kerosene smell and my head hurt from the harsh treatment. I pulled my soft pink flowered nightgown over my head. There was a foggy mirror in the room and I secretly admired my reflection feeling pretty being so clean and fresh.

"Let me show you your room," Mrs. Humiston said softly. "With you here there are ten girls, twenty two children in all."

I followed quietly listening as she talked but remaining silent. We climbed the dark narrow stairway, the light from the lantern flickering on the walls making strange shapes and dancing wildly as we climbed the creaky stairs. The wind howled mournfully around the house goosebumps stood up on my arm and I shivered. We finally arrived at the large girls' bedroom.

The beds lined the walls, girls sleeping peacefully, the occasional snore breaking the silence. Mrs. Humiston showed me a neatly made bed and indicated that's where I could sleep. The bed was covered in a quilt made from brown, red and orange fabric pieces. I shoved my tattered suitcase under the bed and crawled under the quilt. I shivered, the room was cool, everything seemed so strange. Mrs. Humiston tucked me in and whispered a gentle good night. She then turned and left the room, closing the door with a gentle click.

I lay there a long time, thinking of the past few days hearing the unfamiliar creaking of the house. Unknown noises that I couldn't recognize, kept me from sleep, an owl hooted his lonely call from a nearby tree. Thoughts churned in my head until complete exhaustion took over, and I fell asleep. My deep breathing and gentle snores joined the girls as we slept the night away.

Chapter 9

I woke early the following morning, from my bed, the sun had just risen and was splashing pink and purple fingers of light over the distant horizon. The sky was clear and brilliant, promising a beautiful day.

I sleepily glanced around the room, most of the beds had two sleeping girls, still asleep. Assorted quilts covered the beds with a variety of colors and patterns from bright reds and yellows to dark navy blues and browns. I had a bed to myself which I was thankful for.

Hooks hung on the walls by our beds for dresses, on the left of the hooks stood sturdy dressers made from dark wood. The dressers had round black knobs to open the drawers. Mrs. Humiston had told me yesterday that each girl could use a drawer for her under things and other personal items if she had.

In a corner of the room, was a washstand with a large mottled blue tin pitcher and matching bowl. The bowl and the pitcher were both chipped in several areas and looked well used. Hanging on one of the hooks was a worn chocolate brown towel, for our hands and faces.

I looked around the room at the girls still sleeping, most appearing older than me. One girl who appeared my age was awake and gazing seriously at me, her thick ebony colored hair was a wild mass all over her head. She had intense, sparkling hazel eyes framed with long dark lashes, her lips were red and full. Her skin was the color of coffee with cream in it, I thought she was very pretty and gave her a shy smile. Her face lit up bright like the sun, grinning she said.

"My name is Edna and I am seven."

As she spoke the clear ring of a cowbell started to dong, the music echoing through the house and sending its chimes into the great outdoors. I sat up quickly, my eyes wide in alarm, unsure of what was happening.

"We need to get up and get ready for breakfast in a half hour, and make our bed and wash our faces," Edna chatted happily. She took the edge of my quilt and pulled it to cover the pillow, reaching for the other side. I straightened it so it lay smooth on the straw mattress. I then helped her with her bed making sure the corners were straight like Miss Emma had taught me.

"I was hoping a girl my age would move in here," Edna said enthusiastically. "Most of the girls are older and act as if I am a baby." She scowled momentarily and looked sad and her pink bottom lip stuck out a bit.

"I can be your friend," I said quietly with a shy smile. "I like you."

Edna grinned widely showing two missing front teeth. "I like you too." She gave me a quick hug. "Let's hurry and get dressed so we can have breakfast."

We pulled our dresses over our heads. We then helped each other with our buttons that we had on the back of our dresses.

Edna wanted to comb my hair so I let her. She combed my blonde hair gently trying to make two braids but she didn't know how so she just tied it with a ribbon. My hair stuck up everywhere. We giggled when we looked in the mirror. Then grabbing each other's hands we bounded down the stairs.

The wood table was set with tin ware dishes and cutlery. I counted twenty two place settings. The table stretched across the room and it appeared that breakfast was ready and waiting.

For breakfast we had warm oatmeal with a little brown sugar and milk. It was so good.

After breakfast, Mrs. Humiston came to me. She gave a gentle squeeze and asked me how I had slept.

"Good," I said suddenly, feeling shy.

She smiled kindly. "Everyone has to help out here," she stated matter-of-factly as she quickly brushed out my hair and made two tight braids tying it tightly with a red ribbon. "Your duty this week is to help in the kitchen. You'll need to help with dishes, peel potatoes, or whatever is needed. You can start after school this afternoon." She gave me a little pat on my shoulder.

"Now get going, you need to get to school." She grinned and winked.

Edna and I walked to the schoolhouse, skipping as we swung our lunch pails, braids bouncing wildly. The schoolhouse was a small building behind a large house that was the orphanage.

A tall and broad shouldered man with rough calloused hands met us at the door. His wavy blonde hair curled around his ears and a moustache with long sideburns.

"Good morning, young ladies," he said in a stately voice.

"Edna, it looks like you brought a friend, can you introduce her?"

"This is Bella, she's my new best friend. She moved here yesterday." Edna was beaming at me as she spoke.

"Nice to meet you, I am Mr. Hutchens, your teacher. You can sit with Edna."

Edna half dragged me in her eagerness to her seat. The bench was a well-worn plank with a small sort of table attached to the back seat in front of us.

We said the Lord's Prayer in unison, then sang the national anthem. Mr. Hutchens led the singing with his deep musical voice. I didn't know either very well, but I will practice so I can know them off by heart.

After the singing we sat down again and the teacher gave us our arithmetic assignment. I sat quietly and paid close attention when the teacher spoke. He gave me a slate to do my work on, it's black and Mr. Hutchens said that slate is made of stone. It is a rectangular shape with wooden edges, someone has carved swirls and lines on it with a carving knife. I worked hard on my numbers and did my arithmetic neatly.

Later, after recess, I started learning about vowels and consonants and the sound they make when they slide into each other. The sounds we learned were b, a, t, bat, and other three letter words. I had learned this already so this was easy for me.

At lunchtime Edna and I, and a few other girls sat on the grass outside and ate our lard sandwiches. As we chatted and laughed the breeze teased our hair and the strands blew in our eyes. The day was warm and the sun warmed my face and I relaxed in the presence of new friends.

When we were finished, we put our lunch pails away on the shelf above the hooks for our outerwear. Then we raced to the pump taking turns pumping the rusty handle until we filled a bucket of water. When the bucket was filled, we used the water dipper and drank our fill, giving the dipper to the next one in line.

After our lunch, we studied geography, which is learning about different places and cultures.

After school we went back to the orphanage, had a small snack, and then we had to do our chores. I was on kitchen duty and I was assigned to peel potatoes. There was a huge pile of red potatoes, although I had never peeled potatoes before I wanted to do my chores. I was given a small paring knife and tried peeling the peel off thinly. I accidentally nicked my thumb and it started to bleed, I shook my thumb and the blood sprayed on the peeled potatoes, but I ignored the bleeding and quickly finished the rest of the potatoes. I had discreetly slipped potato peels in my apron pocket so I could eat later. When the peeling was finished I handed the peeled potatoes in a pail to Mrs. Humiston.

She quickly glanced at the potatoes and her eyes widened in horror.

Seeing her look I bowed my head in shame. "I'm sorry," I said quietly, "I did the best I could."

Before I had even finished speaking, she reached for my hand and she gently picked it up and looked at my still bleeding thumb. Putting her arm around my shoulder she scurried me over to a pitcher of water. After cleaning it, she wrapped a small rag around my thumb to stop the bleeding.

Mrs. Humiston then gave me a quick hug and a kiss on the forehead and informed me that I had done well and that I should let her know if it happened again right away.

Since I had been excused, I sat on the small porch and watched the boys cut up firewood. The breeze playfully lifted the strands of hair around my face. The sun gently shone down and hugged my body with its warmth.

I did not sit long as Mrs. Humiston asked if I wanted to ring the cowbell for supper and of course I was very enthusiastic. Children came from all corners of the yard and house, to wash up at the pump, and then head for the table.

After supper and dishes were finished, we were allowed to play outside for a while. Edna and I and a few others played with dolls under the great oak tree in the backyard. When the sun's rays were kissing the western horizon good night with glorious colors, the bell rang again. It was bedtime and another day was over.

Life fell into a predictable routine and I began to love my new home and friends.

Every Friday afternoon there is a spelling bee at school. Edna and I study hard, we try to do better than each other, it's a lot of fun.

At recess we play games like softball or kick the can. The boys sometimes would play marbles, us girls played with dolls or skipping games.

After school, I help with supper preparation, washing and setting the table, peeling potatoes, and putting dishes away. The head cook is teaching me how to make cornbread. There's a lot of girls helping so we get our work done quickly.

On cleaning duty I dust the furniture, sweep and mop the main room floors. The bedrooms just get swept on the weekdays. It is our responsibility to hang up our own clothes and keep our beds made neatly.

The stove in the kitchen has the ashes removed daily, we dump the ashes in the outhouse holes, it takes the bad smells away.

When I am doing laundry I scrub the smaller items on a board that's called a scrub board, I stick it in a cast iron tub and scrub, until the item is clean, then hang them up on the line outside. The sun makes them bright and crisp, the fresh air makes them smell fresh and clean.

The next day we iron the sheets, shirts and dresses and even our underwear. The iron is heated on the stove, when it's hot we iron out all the wrinkles. I once tried to iron a sheet, the iron was too hot and burned the sheet with a brown mark in the shape of the iron, I was more careful after that. The ironing is hot work as the fire in the stove is burning, even on warm days. It's my least favorite job to do.

On Saturdays, we clean the fireplaces and the stove, we scrub blacking on the stove to make it shiny and remove any leftover grease and splatters. We also take the stove pipes and scrub them on the inside to remove the ashes. It's a lot of work but it looks good when we are finished.

After supper, when we're finished with our jobs, we can go play outside. Edna and I love to play with our dolls under the oak tree. Sometimes, other girls join us. We pretend we are teachers and we are teaching the dolls to read. The air is fresh and the rich smell of freshly dug dirt, where the garden was recently planted, reaches our noses. Birds sing merrily and flutter about looking for food for their little ones.

We celebrated Memorial Day on the twenty-eighth day in May. There was a parade, the drummer in the lead, pounding out the rhythm of 'My Country tis of thee' and 'The Star-Spangled Banner.'

Next came the soldiers in their grey worn uniforms, some missing arms or legs, bodies and faces scarred. Their eyes showed the pain and trauma of the war as they marched somberly, to the steady beat of the drums.

Following the drummers was Mrs. Humiston and her three children Franklin, Alice and Frederick, the rest of us children came next, smiling, our arms filled with fragrant flowers, donated by the townsfolk.

Behind us, were people in carriages, walking or on horseback as we made our way up to Cemetery Hill. The villagers of Gettysburg and surrounding towns came for the memorial of the fallen soldiers.

Our trek stopped at the cemetery, the tombstones and white crosses in neatrows surrounding us. We had worked hard scrubbing the tombstones, until they shone, and repainting the crosses.

The atmosphere was sober, even the skies were grey and the breeze cool, as stood on the hillside, in memory of those who gave their life for the war, those who had gone before us.

There was a lengthy speech made by a man wearing a long black coat, grey hair, with little on the top of his head, his beard was full and reached to his crisply ironed collar. He spoke about the men who had sacrificed their lives in a flat monotonous tone and seemed to go on endlessly.

I started thinking about Pa, Mother and my little baby brother whom I never got to know. I cried with the loss, my tears watering the flowers in my hands. Edna reached over and held onto my hand. She smiled at me and I gave her one back, immediately feeling better.

After the speech we stood at attention with our hand over our hearts as we sang the national anthem, our voices carrying over the hillside and down to the valley.

Then we, the children from the orphanage, sprinkled flowers over the soldier's graves. The graves of some of the children's fathers, uncles and even brothers, now lay cold beneath the ground. Edna's parents were both buried there, having passed years ago. Tears were shed, we made sure no cross or tombstone was missed, all was adorned with flowers.

Mrs. Humiston and the children on kitchen duty this week, had made a picnic lunch for us: fried chicken, potato salad, carrot sticks and apple pie. It was delicious. We sat on the hill, our feet bare among the whispering grass and blooming wildflowers. The sun came out from behind the clouds and smiled gently down on us. We were allowed the day off from chores and we played until the sun went down on the horizon filling the sky with glowing ray's in various hues of color. Tired from climbing trees, playing with dolls, hide and seek, we headed for the house. As tomorrow was Sunday, we had our weekly bath, before sleepily crawling into our cozy beds. The sweet memories of the day filled my dreams with joy and laughter.

Chapter 10

The next day was Sunday and we got dressed into our best clothes. I wore my beautiful soft blue church dress that Miss Emma had sewn for me. It seemed so long ago I had stayed with her, so many changes since then. The dress emphasized my eyes and they shone with happiness.

Edna and I walked joyfully to the local church, swinging our hands and dancing a few steps as we sang songs we had learned from school. Miss Humiston had to remind us to be calm and to keep our clothes tidy. We did try to calm down, we then held hands and whispered to each other about school and the other children.

The church had rows of hard wooden benches, smoothed from the wear of parishioners who sat, listening to the gospel, through the years. They lined both sides of the church, in the middle in the front was the wooden pulpit where the preacher lay his Bible when he preached. The pulpit was approximately five feet high and enclosed on three sides. There was a sort of a table on top where the Bible rested. Inside were shelves where they kept the communion cups. The preacher stood behind the pulpit. He opened his well-worn Bible, read and spoke on the verses.

We sat at the back of the church. I sat beside Edna with Mrs. Humiston sat farther down the bench. The other children filled the benches behind and in front of us.

The preacher was tall and thin, his neatly pressed clothes looked tired as they had seen better days. His eyes were deep-set and a dark, rich brown, hair was thinning and parted on the side, combed neatly.

He spoke earnestly yet compassionately, on Jesus healing the broken hearted, that He loved us and that we should come to Him. He died for us so we could heal from our trauma. From losing our parents or the many different things that people can say to hurt us, He loves the brokenhearted and wants to help us. I listened intently for a while, I didn't understand everything he spoke about.

My mind started to wander and I imagined myself as a schoolteacher. I would teach my students their numbers and letters, I was so lost in thought that I didn't realize that the preacher was leading the congregation in prayer, and everyone was standing. Edna poked me and was laughing her hand over her mouth, eyes sparkling with humor.

My face got hot and I rose quickly running my hands down my skirt in an attempt to smooth the wrinkles in my dress with my sweaty palms. I side glanced at Mrs. Humiston to see if she had noticed. Her eyes were closed and her lips moved as if she was praying. I breathed a sigh of relief.

We finished the service singing,

"What a friend we have in Jesus all our sins and griefs to bear.

"What a privilege to carry everything to God in prayer."

I read the words from the black hymn book and tried to sing along. Mrs. Humiston smiled at me reassuringly and gave me a wink. I grinned back showing my missing front teeth.

The school term was almost finished for the season when we heard the exciting news. The Governor of Pennsylvania John Geary, Ulysses Grant, and some other union generals were coming in June. They wanted to visit our orphanage!

I was excited as we didn't have visitors often. The house was scrubbed from the hot attic to the cold, dark basement.

The garden was growing. We worked hard to keep it free from weeds. We were already eating fresh peas, lettuce and radishes.

The boys used a reel mower, made with large bicycle tires for easy pushing. They cut the lawn with sharp steel blades that turned in a circular motion when pushed by a long handle with handlebars to maneuver the mower easily. It took a day to finish and all the boys had to take a turn with the mowing.

Finally, everything was ready. We all had a bath even if it wasn't Saturday. As many as ten children used the water before it was replaced and got fresh water from the pump. They started with the youngest until they got to the oldest.

The sun rose the next morning, the misty blue sky filling the horizon with pinks, oranges, and yellows in varying shades of light. Birds trilled their clear notes on a sunny morning. Far in the distance geese were honking as they flew north.

The morning dew had evaporated from the freshly cut lawn, when an elegant-looking carriage pulled by matching chestnut horses trotted down the dirt path, winding its majestic way to the homestead. The driver got down and tied the horses securely to the hitching post using a double knot to hold the reins in place. He then opened the carriage door for the men. Four gentlemen in fine suit coats sedately stepped down.

I recognized Governor John Geary as I had seen his picture in the paper. He was a handsome man with chocolate brown eyes and a sturdy nose, his hair was dark brown with just a hint of curls. The hair on his chin was neatly trimmed and the sides of his face were cleanly shaven. John Geary was extremely tall, I craned my neck to look up at his face. I shook his hand and it swallowed my small hand. He towered over the other men and was sturdily built.

I also knew who General Ulysses Grant was. He was a Commanding General in the Union Army. His face was broad and his hair brown, the beard was trimmed neatly sprinkled with grey. His eyes were a stormy blue. He was a whole foot shorter than John Geary.

The other two men I did not know but I was told they were Union Civil War Generals. I was excited when they shook my hand and I told them my name. My heart was beating fast and my palms were sweaty. I tried to act calm and ladylike and gave a curtsy, Mrs. Humiston teaches us manners.

The men were friendly and impressed with the cleanliness and upbeat atmosphere of the home. They discussed the need for adding on to the home and a dorm for the girls.

When the visit was winding down, a professional photographer came to take our picture. The boys stood on the left and the girls on the right. The visitors in the center. There was giggling and a few playful pushes. The boys made strange faces but finally settled down and the photographer was able to take a picture.

After the gentleman left, we had an energetic baseball game. I didn't strike out like I often do and hit the ball it was a day to remember.

It wasn't long after this that a couple came to the orphanage wishing to adopt a girl. The lady had soft blue-grey eyes. They looked kind and the lines on her gentle face were smile lines. Her hair once brown was now streaked with grey. Her flowered purple dress covered a full figure.

Her husband was of average height. His wife's head reached to his shoulders. He was deeply tanned, his hands calloused from years of hard labor. His eyes were an intense sky blue. He wore a green plaid shirt and overalls.

They told Mrs. Humiston that they had been unable to have children. They had always wanted a family but it never happened. Now that they were financially stable, they wanted to give a child a home. They had a few cows, pigs and chickens. They had lots of space for a child to get fresh air and exercise.

As they visited with the children, they fell in love with Edna, and she with them. It didn't take them long to get adoption papers, and Edna now had a new home. I missed her intensely.

Life continued, and seasons passed. I excelled at school applying myself to my grades. I enjoyed living in the home but I did not have a special friend. I got along with just about everybody but I wanted someone with whom I could be best friends.

The orphanage grew until there were close to sixty children. They added more to the original building creating more rooms. The girls had their dorm which was built in the yard.

The year I was ten, two more children came to live at the orphanage. The boy was tall and thin with straggly strawberry blonde hair with light eyebrows over dove grey eyes. His face was narrow and freckles scattered over his nose and cheeks. What was unusual about him is that he had part of his arm missing and no hand on that side.

He walked with a swagger and with his shoulder shoved a boy against the wall. "I'm going to beat you up."

He snarled. The younger boy backed away, stuttering that he didn't want to fight. "I'm watching you!" He growled. "You look like trouble."

The younger boy quickly disappeared from the room.

The girl, Lizzie tossed her auburn curls and rolled her eyes.

"Stop it, Richard," she said in a superior tone. "You promised Mother you wouldn't fight." He glared at his sister and stomped out of the house, slamming the door.

I shyly walked over to Lizzie. "My name is Bella. Do you want to play?" She casually looked me over, her green eyes sparkling.

"Sure, do you know how to play cowboys and Indians?"

"I haven't played that, maybe you can teach us?" I said eagerly. "Who wants to play?"

A chorus of 'Me' and 'I do' filled the room. Lizzie organized us into groups. We had a rowdy game, the rules made up as we went along. The Indians hid and tried to kidnap the cowboys. There was a lot of laughing and we were dusty and tired at the end of the day.

Mrs. Humiston sighed when she saw us and sent us to clean up at the pump in the yard. "I need to teach them to be ladies," she said thoughtfully to herself. She added sewing, cross-stitching or knitting to our schedules for a half hour before bedtime Every Friday, we had a spelling bee and we desperately tried to out spell each other. I was good with spelling and sometimes won the contest.

In winter, we built snow forts and attacked the boys with snowballs. Hiding behind trees and buildings, we let the snowballs fly when they least expected it. Sometimes the boys got us first. We took toboggans and slid down Cemetery Hill.

At Christmas, we went on sleigh rides behind a prancing horse bedecked with bells that jingled merrily in the crisp winter air. We sang Christmas carols loudly and with enthusiasm. We were happy and lived joyfully at the orphanage. Unbeknown to us changes were coming shortly and dark clouds were gathering on the horizon.

Chapter 11

At the end of the year, Mrs. Humiston received a marriage proposal from Mr. Asa Barnes, a retired clergyman and two years her senior. After much deliberation, she agreed to marry him.

I was deeply saddened as I loved her and her daughter Alice. She was a gentle lady who often gave encouraging words or smiles. Her love reached us all at the homestead.

Before the wedding, Mrs. Humiston gave me a notebook as a farewell gift. The book had a plain dark blue cover inside were blank white pages and on them, she had written in neat cursive.

Bella, you are a beautiful girl. Please write your stories, dreams and thoughts, hopefully, one day you will realize the strong, compassionate person you are.
Mrs. Humiston

She reached over and gave me a light squeeze around my shoulders.

"I have a feeling that you'll be facing tough challenges in the future. Have courage, bad times don't last forever."

I hugged her back. My eyes were misty with tears. "I love you and I'm going to miss you."

I sobbed tears trickling down my cheeks and onto her broad shoulders. "I love you too," she murmured.

After they left for their new home, Dr. Bourns, the manager of the orphanage and who was in charge of the finances, hired a new lady to fill Mrs. Humiston's vacated position.

The children animatedly gossiped about the new matron, some wondering if she would be strict or kind like Mrs. Humiston had been. Lizzie was concerned if she would teach Latin and higher-level mathematics, I worried about that too. Lizzie and I were competitive in our schoolwork, each trying to get better grades than the other.

One evening when there was a board meeting at home, I dropped at the office door when Dr. Bourns and the board of directors were discussing her application.

"She comes highly recommended and has few equals," a deep voice was saying. I recognized it as Mr. Stewart's one of the board members. "She is an assiduous and faithful worker."

Straining, I tried to listen to the conversation. Hearing children's footsteps pounding rapidly down the hallway in my direction, I swiftly crept away before I was caught.

I did not know what the word assiduous meant but it sounded like it was a good thing to be. I anticipated Miss Carmichael's arrival with eagerness.

Miss Rosa Carmichael was of average height. Her dark brown hair was combed severely down with a braid on the top of her head. Her cheeks were full and her eyes hazel. Her gaze is serious, lips thin with frown wrinkles around her mouth and eyes. Her figure was slim with wide hips.

Things slowly started to change after she arrived. She loved order and believed the children lacked discipline. We were instructed to file into the dining room in a calm orderly manner. If anyone was caught not listening, talking or misbehaving they were banned from their rooms.

The rule that children were to be seen and not heard was strictly enforced.

Talking at the table was not permitted. Miss Carmichael dished out our miserly food portions. We were not allowed to ask for salt, water or anything we may require. Chewing loudly, with the mouth open, having food on our face, burping or any other misdemeanor called for consequences as she felt fit to dole out. It often was a smack on the cheek with her hand.

Occasionally she used a belt or wooden spoon.

She called us heathens and barbarians and worried it was too late to change our evil ways, fearing the fires of hell on our poor wicked souls.

Dr. Bourns came over more often during the summer. We were forced to serve him by preparing food, polishing his shoes, washing and ironing his laundry and doing whatever he required of us. We worked hard to take care of his many demands, this was along with our never-ending list of jobs to do around the house. If we did not work fast enough or do a satisfactory job we would get slapped by Miss Carmichael.

Richard's anger and aggression slowly increased in the following months. At first, he just shoved and wrestled with the boys. One morning he shoved a small girl out of his way, she fell and skinned her knee, and started to cry.

I was right behind her, and I slapped him with all my strength yelling, "Leave her alone!" He then grabbed my hair and pulled it down. I seized his arm and bit, leaving teeth marks.

Miss Carmichael seeing the fight, gripped my ears and dragged me away from Richard. Quickly, I did a well-aimed kick to his shins.

She vehemently scolded me saying, I was a heathen and would come to a bad end shaking me viciously.

I protested loudly, "It was Richard's fault, he hit Jessie."

Miss Carmichael whipped around and slapped my cheek leaving the imprint of her hand on my face. Tears pooled in my eyes but I refused to cry.

"Don't talk back to me," she roared. She forcibly pulled me to the basement and with a rough push, I landed hard on the cement floor, skinning my hands and knees. Grabbing my hands roughly, she forcibly put them in shackles locking them and dropping the key in her apron pocket. The basement was dark and gloomy, I was in a small room that had originally been used for cold storage. Mice skittered around looking for food. A small snake slithered into my view and I shuddered in fear. The darkness surrounded me, suffocating the air damp and smelling of mound. I shivered but was unable to warm myself. The minutes and then hours dragged on, without food or water. Alone. I yelled and struggled against the shackles but it was of no use. Fighting just caused them to rub against the iron and my wrists began to bleed. After a while, I had to use the outhouse and was in agony, unable to hold it any longer and I wet myself. It was sticky and smelly sitting in my water. When Miss Carmichael later found out she beat me with a wooden spoon.

Lizzie and I discussed it in whispers after going to bed. Richard had not been reproved for his part in the tussle. Lizzie believed that Miss Carmichael had observed what he had done to Jessie.

We questioned if Miss Carmichael's belief in a vengeful God is true. Lizzie stated that her mother taught her that God was loving and desired everyone to be saved. I was not sure about how I felt about God and all the different ways that people believed he was like. I put this in the back of my mind and pondered on it later.

School attendance had become sporadic and only if Miss Carmichael believed we had behaved appropriately. She had let Mr. Hutchens go, and she now taught the classes.

One day a young girl, Aimee, was struggling with her fractions in arithmetic. Miss Carmichael was annoyed and angrily retorted that she wasn't trying. Aimee insisted tearfully that she was.

Miss Carmichael slapped her hard for answering back, then commanded Aimee to stand on top of her desk, she started to cry harder, her shoulders heaving as tears spilled from her eyes.

Miss Carmichael grabbed a yardstick and hit Aimee on her legs and welts instantly appeared. She started to scream in terror, eyes wide in fear. She crawled on top of her desk, her legs trembling. Standing on the desk, her body shook.

"Don't move," Miss Carmichael snarled, "or I'll whip you." Aimee stiffened doing her best to stand straight.

We watched in horror. The smaller children cried softly into their sodden handkerchiefs. One of the older boys had his fists clenched, his lips in a tight narrow slash. His eyes flashed fire and hate.

Lizzie and I sat unmoving, bodies tense in fear, praying that Miss Carmichael wouldnot hurt Aimee or anyone else. I gave a swift glance to Lizzie, her face was white and her eyes were wide.

I snuck a look at Richard. He was slouched at his desk, eyes were half-closed and a smug smirk lazily crossed his lips. He appeared to be enjoying the drama.

I suddenly was filled with red hot rage clenching my fists. I took a deep breath knowing that if I let out my anger others would get hurt biting my lip, hard to keep from saying anything, tasting blood on my tongue. I had to remain calm and keep myself in control. Taking deep slow breaths I allowed the anger to slip away. It was replaced with sadness and fear.

Why was she acting this way? Would things get better or would they get worse? Would I have the strength if it got worse?

"Get back to work," Miss Carmichael snapped. Her sharp voice sliced through my dark thoughts.

There was a rustling of pages as in panic we tried to find our place in our textbook. We worked in silence. The scratchy noise of our chalks on our slates was the only sound in the room.

We were terrified to anger her more than she already was. Aimee stood exhausted as we watched her, she looked as if she would collapse.

Finally, after hours of standing, she was permitted to get down. She was weak and limp, the older girls had to half carry her into the house. She leaned heavily on them. Her body shook like a leaf, her legs trembled, and her strength was gone.

I snuck into her room later and gave her a bun from supper. I had stuffed it into my apron pocket. Her body was still shivering and she had a headache. She had vomited previously. When I was visiting Aimee, Miss Carmichael entered the room. Quickly, I crawled under the bed. It was a tight squeeze but luckily wasn't caught.

Miss Carmichael spoke to Aimee for a long time about rebellion as the sin of witchcraft. That she was going to hell if she didn't change. She scolded for what felt like a long time. Her harsh voice was like fingernails on a slate, scratchy and irritating.

Aimee was crying softly, her head on her knees a desolate figure on the bed. Her hand swiped at the tears sliding down her cheeks. Finally, Miss Carmichael left, when her footsteps hit the creaky board on the stairs, I crawled from under the bed. My legs and back were cramped from being squeezed under the bed for so long.

My heart hurt for Aimee. She was only eight and small for her age and didn't deserve the mistreatment that had been doled out to her today. I hugged her before I pensively, with head down and hands behind my back made my way to my bed. I was deep in thought about Miss Carmichael's actions today and her ideas about what she believes are rebellion. "Why was Miss Carmichael so cruel? Are we that sinful and rebellious?" I pondered. I thought about it until late that night. I did not come to a satisfactory conclusion.

When the lights were out, Lizzie and I talked in whispers about the good times with Mrs. Humiston. We fondly remembered playing outside, picnics and lots of other fun activities.

Mrs. Humiston had never warned us of the evils but taught us with kindness and patience. Thinking of those memories I thought that I would rather be kind like Mrs. Humiston than harsh like Miss Carmichael. I promised myself to be more compassionate in my interactions with the children and make their lives easier. I told myself that it was time for me to grow up.

Chapter 12

Spring returned with radiant sunrises, honking of geese flying overhead, cool crisp breeze and the smells of freshly hoed dirt and whatever fragrances the wind brought. Fawns on wobbly legs searched out the green shoots in the fields with their mother's ways protectively on guard. Farmers started calving season and baby calves, lambs and foals frolicked in the greening meadows.

With spring here again we started with the plans to celebrate Memorial Day. Every year since the orphanage opened we have been in a parade, had a picnic and put fresh flowers on our father's and the fallen soldier's graves.

We talked in hushed tones, excitedly planning the day. We were hoping for sunshine and wondering what to pack for the picnic lunch. Our joy was dashed in pieces when Miss Carmichael, with hands on her hips and her eyes cold, informed us that we would not be participating this year. She stated that our behavior in the last year did not warrant this privilege.

I could see the hurt and disappointment in the children's eyes. We knew better than to say anything but I reached for Lizzie's hand and gave it a gentle squeeze. Our eyes met for a moment and we shot unsaid words of bitterness to the other.

One small boy named Elmer, who hadn't been here long, started to sob. I reached for him but was not quick enough.

Miss Carmichael grabbed him roughly by his arm and shook him demanding that he stop crying. His eyes widened in fear, his cries coming in gasps as he tried to stifle his tears. Miss Carmichael then dragged him, his legs flailing wildly screaming in protest and horror. Elmer struggled valiantly but she was stronger and he was hauled to the rain barrel which was overflowing with the recent spring rains. His terror-filled screams were blood-curdling and my hair stood on end in fear for his safety. My eyes showed my horror, as he was liftedroughly and then dumped savagely into the rain barrel.

Miss Carmichael aggressively pushed his head under the water and held him down for what seemed like forever but may have only been a couple of minutes. When she released her grip l he came to the surface sputtering and choking, murky water spraying on the onlookers.

The children cringed and shrank back in terror, eyes wide in horror. The little ones trembled in fright and a few started silently crying, huddled together for protection.

One of the bigger boys stepped forward and reached for Elmer. Miss Carmichael slapped him so hard that he fell to his knees on the ground. The boy looked angry at having been hit yet powerless to assist the small boy.

"Leave the disciplining to me," she snarled. "Go to your room for the rest of the day."

The boy turned and slowly walked to the house, his face dejected and sad. Helplessness slumped his shoulders as he closed the door behind him.

I was incapable of helping my heart thudded painfully against my chest. Tears leaked from my eyes and a feeling of vulnerability swept over me like a flood.

"There's nothing I can do. I need to do something!" Utter desperation filled my body. My shoulders slumped in despair. We children could not control the situation. We were forced to live with this horrible cruel woman. What would she think up next?

Grabbing the edge of the barrel, fingernails digging into the wood, Elmer frantically pulled himself up and with his arms extended he was able to keep himself from sinking to the bottom.

There was a cool spring breeze that morning and Elmer shivered uncontrollably, his lips turning blue and his face had a mottled appearance from the cold.

Miss Carmichael stood erectly with a tight-lipped smile, her dark brown hair in its severe bun coming loose in tangled strands, eyes fierce and calculating, she looked wild and a little crazy. It scared me and instinctively took a small step backwards.

My heart pounded anxiously, when would she let him out of the rain barrel? After what seemed like a long time, she grabbed the limp boy, who was now weak from exhaustion, digging her fingernails into his armpits, lifted him and tossed him, like a bag of potatoes, on the hard-packed dirt.

"Hopefully that will teach you not to disagree with my authority." She snapped harshly. Turning abruptly, she marched back straight, head held high into the house and slammed the door.

I glanced around cautiously and when it appeared safe, crept my way slowly to Elmer as he lay in a wet huddled heap. Kneeling before him I heaved him into my arms. I had grown lately and was thin, but strong. Struggling to carry him into the house, I panted for breath.

From the corner of my eye, I noticed Richard saunter around the house. My heart raced and my hands grew clammy. My thoughts filled with anxiety, what would he do? Would he hurt me? Would he tell Miss Carmichael?

He said nothing, his eyes flitted around the yard and then awkwardly opened the door for me. He avoided eye contact and scurried away when I whispered a soft "Thank you."

I carried Elmer to his bedroom and dried him off with a small towel, rubbing him until his color returned to a pinkish hue. After searching through his worn clothes I found a threadbare pair of pants with a ragged rip in the knee. I put them on him, hanging his damp clothes on his bed frame.

I tucked him in and placed a kiss on his cheek. Elmer reached up with his arms and gave me a tight hug, his tears dripping on my blouse. I hugged him back wiping the tears from his face with my hand. Speaking gently I encouraged him to rest. He nodded in agreement. I tiptoed out of the room thankful I had not been caught.

Memorial Day was a damp day. The skies seemed to weep for us as it drizzled steadily. We stood in a wet bedraggled group with our worn and patched clothes, our faces were sad and dejected with the loss of the privilege to put flowers on the graves. We watched as the town children placed flowers on our father's and the soldiers' graves.

I could barely remember my family anymore. Tears trickled down my face as I felt the intense loss of not having a family. Lizzie, noticing my tears cautiously maneuvered her way over to me. She stood in silent support beside me. When no one was looking she gave a light touch on my arm and a sympathetic smile.

The townspeople were unhappy that the orphan children were not involved in the Memorial Day activities. We had looked so forlorn and uncared for, they had been hearing stories of mistreatment and abuse at the orphanage. The board visited us but gave Miss Carmichael notice, she hid the children that were the most mistreated and bruised, making sure they would not be seen.

As soon as the visitors left the beatings and being locked up would start up again in full force even worse than before. Once again crying and screams would be heard throughout the orphanage and the outbuildings in the yard.

Miss Carmichael had vehemently denied all the allegations. She stated coldly that the talk was slanderous and she only had the children's best interest in mind.

The visit seemed to increase her vigilance on us and was quick to pounce on any misdemeanor no matter how small. We never knew when she would find fault. She refused to let us attend school or church services saying we were incorrigible.

Chapter 13

I have been growing a lot in the last few months. My dresses are below the knee not at the ankle like a woman would wear. Miss Carmichael has not allowed me to get new clothes even though I finally have a woman's figure. My freckles have almost completely disappeared.

Lizzie matured earlier than I have and is shorter than me and curvier. I think she is beautiful with her wavy auburn hair and her bright green eyes and the splattering of freckles on her nose.

On one of those many long dreary days as I was scrubbing the floor, I began to have sharp stabbing pain in my stomach area. My head throbbed with a headache and there was a dull ache in my lower back. I wasn't feeling well at all that day.

Miss Carmichael was in an exceptionally foul mood, she had children locked in their rooms and throughout the day I could hear children getting hit and the cries of pain she inflicted on them.

She came around the kitchen door just in time to see me rubbing my back and accused me of being lazy. She then called two of the older boys to assist her. I started crying when she grabbed me by the arm pleading with her not to punish me. I had a sore back and wasn't feeling good. My protests were unheard of. The boys grabbed my feet and Miss Carmichael had my arms and they dragged me into the basement. I scratched, kicked and yelled as I bumped rudely down the narrow wooden stairs.

They forced me into the shackles and with the boys holding me down, shackled my hands to the wall. Then they left me alone in the basement. My hair hung limply on my sweaty face, arms and legs were sore and bruised.

The basement was chilly and the room was filled with darkness. There was a skittering noise as something moved about the enclosed room. My heart raced, thumping loudly, and my palms grew sweaty. My eyes slowly adjusted and I could see that it was a mouse searching for food for her babies.

The pain in my stomach had become unbearable and I could feel wetness running down my legs. I pulled my legs up to my chest and it slightly eased the pain. Glancing down my eyes widened in horror. I was bleeding internally!

"I am dying," I thought in panic. I'm shackled to a wall and my life is over. My head dropped to my knees. I cried hysterically with deep racking sobs. My body shook with fear. Finally, weak with exhaustion, my hands hanging from the chains a wisp of memory came sneaking into my thoughts.

Many years ago, I was in church and a young clergyman was preaching. I wished I would have listened. Closing my eyes, I breathed in deeply. The memory returned bringing a sense of peace.

As my spirit calmed, the words that had been spoken came to me.

"He hath sent me to bind up the brokenhearted, to proclaim liberty to the captives, and to open up the prison to those that are bound."

I recalled that he spoke of a man named Jesus. I was bound to this wall. I was broken-hearted. Could Jesus heal my brokenheart?

In the recesses of my mind, a song returned to me that they had sung in church that long-ago day, and I started humming.

"What a friend we have in Jesus, All our sins and griefs to bear.

"What a privilege to carry, Everything to God in prayer."

Did I have grief and burdens? Yes, I did. I cried at night, feeling overwhelmed by the abuse the children and I experienced. I could do very little to protect them as I was so often locked in my room or basement.

The thought stayed with me persisting that Jesus wanted to be my friend. He wanted to carry my burden. He was not out to condemn me to hell as Miss Carmichael taught.

Jesus loved me. Me! Alone, forsaken orphan with no one. Jesus loved and cared for me. A warmth spread over my being.

"Jesus," I prayed, "I want you to be my friend please help me, and I want to be your friend too."

Soft healing tears rolled down my cheeks. They seemed to cleanse my soul, making me feel fresh and new.

Joy filled my heart and spread throughout me. Jesus was my friend! I wanted to share his friendship with the children around me.

I closed my eyes and with a contented sigh, leaned back against the cold wall to wait for the end of my punishment.

When I was finally released from the basement, Lizzie gave me a gentle back rub and tried encouraging me with soothing words.

I told her about the blood I was losing. She explained that it happens to all girls when they become women and it would happen every month.

I was not pleased with this news. She showed me how to fold rags to control the flow of blood. I'm thankful for my friend, Lizzie.

Our clothes were worn and faded and we had no shoes. We ate once a day and we were used to hunger pains. Rarely were we allowed taking baths because of the need to save water. Sometimes the strong body odors were almost unbearable and the stench would burn my eyes.

Miss Carmichael gave me the most menial jobs. I was instructed to wash and put a blackening paint on the stove. She demanded perfection and it had to be blackened to her satisfaction. I also cleaned the stovepipes. Using a wire brush I scrubbed the inside until it was free from rust and ashes. I also emptied the chamber pots from under the beds into the outhouse holes. After my job was finished for the day, she locked me in my bedroom.

I often felt hopeless and despaired of ever getting out of the orphanage. My feelings were like a dark cloud and I felt that they would suffocate me. I struggled with being positive but it was difficult.

Lizzie and I had many long talks. When we struggled with depression, we tried to encourage each other. Eventually, we would be too old for the orphanage. We looked forward to those days. It seemed that it was very far in the future.

Lizzie and I had grown protective of the little ones. We did what we could to keep them from Miss Carmichael's wrath. We often felt so helpless.

During those days, I clung to the thought that Jesus was my friend. When I thought of him my spirit calmed. It gave me the courage to face another day.

I also took these times to write in my notebook. I began with my earliest memories.

Relieving the memories made me realize that I was a survivor. I was strong. I will get through this. I was young and eventually, I believed that I would be free from Miss Carmichael's tyranny. I reminded myself that I was loved.

One cool spring morning, Miss Carmichael declared that Lizzie and I were to dig a hole for the outhouse. I was relieved to have a break from my locked stuffy room.

The lawn was turning into shades of green replacing the brown dead grasses of last year. A chickadee flew anxiously around us. Her nest and babies were safely hidden in the new leaves of the magnificent maple.

I inhaled the fresh spring air. Breathing deeply of the freshly turned dirt of the garden. I listened to the birds trilling their mating calls. Spring was a time of new beginnings and I was feeling the faint whispers of hope.

The ground was cold and the dirt packed hard. We started to dig and even if the work was hard we began to make progress. When the hole was a few feet deep I climbed in and shoveled the dirt up to Lizzie.

As I bent over to dig deeper, I accidentally stepped on my skirt and there was a sound of ripping cloth. I looked down and there was a jagged tear in my skirt.

"Oh no," I groaned. "Miss Carmichael will beat me!"

Lizzie was sympathetic. "I hope your punishment won't be too harsh." She worried; her face lined with concern.

We could not change the fact that my dress was ripped so we toiled all day. Sweat dripped from our faces, muscles ached and our bodies were weak with exhaustion and lack of nourishment.

When the sky behind us was splashed with muted shades of orange, pink and blue our work was completed. I was pleased with how much we were able to accomplish.

"Let me put this away for you," Lizzie said as she reached for my shovel. I nodded in agreement as she headed in the direction of the shed.

I jogged toward the water pump to wash up. Suddenly, I heard moaning as if Lizzie was in pain. Turning I raced to Lizzie and found her gazing in horror at her ripped sleeve. The threadbare material was hanging half off her bodice. Her shoulder was exposed. The material was so thin it tore like paper.

"What am I to do?" She wailed, tears sprouting from her soft green eyes. "I tore it on that nail." Pointing in the direction of a rusty nail on the wall.

Before I could respond, Miss Carmichael returned to inspect our work. She flew into a rage when she noticed our dresses.

"You careless girls, you have no sense of decency looking like that. I have bent over backwards to raise you into ladies but you refuse to cooperate! You both are hopeless and nothing good will come of you," she railed.

Grabbing a stick lying nearby she whacked us hard on our backs, hitting Lizzie so hard the stick broke in half.

"You wicked girls, go straight to your room, I'll be there shortly," she yelled, her face red in rage.

We exchanged glances of sheer panic. We grabbed onto each other's hands when out of her view. The other children huddled in small packs afraid her anger would be redirected at them.

When she came to our room she was carrying two sets of men's clothing.

"Useless girls who can't keep themselves decent, wear men's clothes." Commanding us to change into the clothing.

Lizzie and I exchanged discreet glances showing the disgust we felt at our punishment.

The blue plaid shirt and rough-looking pants hung limply on me as I was thin. I had a black belt tied around my waist to keep the pants up.

Lizzie was curvier than I and her pants and shirt fit more closely to her body. Lizzie was a bit self-conscious about her changing body and she felt very uncomfortable in the men's clothing. She looked at me in anguish, tears filling her eyes. Tears filled my eyes as well but I refused to give Miss Carmichael the satisfaction of knowing how upset we were.

I gave a wobbly smile trying my best to give Lizzie courage and myself as well.

The little children stared at us and the older girls looked at us in pity and compassion. A bigger boy looked upset with the injustice of our punishment. A few boys snickered behind their hands.

I felt exposed. I was used to the full skirts and blouses that men's clothingseemed positively immodest. I remained calm on the outside but inside I was ashamed of my outfit. I see with rage my heart filled with anger and humiliation. Why would Miss Carmichael make us wear men's clothes? The humiliation was real.

Eventually, things settled and the children got used to us wearing men's pants. I was frustrated with the situation and struggled to forgive her, some days it felt impossible. We wore those clothes for two months.

One calm evening as the moon was partially hidden in smoke-colored clouds, the final sunset rays faded in the east, Miss Carmichael checked to see if we had finished our chores.

Henry, a small lad of four or five, had forgotten to bring out the kitchen scraps and dump them in the compost pile. He cried and begged with the promise to finish his work. She refused and said he'd never learn if he got away with the disobedience. Taking his hand, she brought him to the outhouse, after shoving him inside she locked him in.

Turning to us, she reminded us of the importance of immediate obedience andthe consequence of not listening. She demanded that we go straight to our rooms and get to bed.

The younger children scurried away in fear. Anxious that she may turn her anger on to them. I was unwilling to as my heart ached for the little boy. When I lingered, Miss Carmichael, threatened to lock me in the basement. Slowly I moved towards the house. Henry's pitiful wails rang in my ears.

The boy grew hysterical, but after a while, he was able to calm himself. His sobs subsided and loud hiccups shook his small body. He was silent for a while but suddenly we heard piercing screams. The crying shook me to my core. He must be terrified alone in the dark smelly outhouse.

"What had happened to scare him?"

I lay awake worrying for the small child. He was all alone except for spiders, bugs and that awful stench. I knew that Henry had a terrible fear of spiders.

I had dozed off when I was jerked from my sleep. Confused at first about what had woken me I sat up in bed. Then I heard it again. Someone was vehemently knocking on the front door. They were determined to enter, and I heard loud men's voices yelling demanding someone to open the door. I slumped down in my bed and covered my head. My heart raced and my hands grew clammy. I could sense the tension in the air as the pounding continued. We feared the intruder and our imagination filled us with what could happen to us.

I finally heard Miss Carmichael's heavy footsteps shuffle heavily down the hall to the door. I made out two deep men's voices and Miss Carmichael's low voice replying. I strained to hear what was being said but was unable to make out the words. After a lengthy discussion, the men finally left.

The men had been walking past in the middle of the night and had heard Henry screams for help from the locked outhouse. They opened the locked door to see in horror a young boy shivering in the cool air, eyes wide in terror. His face was blotchy from crying, and his nose and eyes dripped. It had taken a long time but the men were able to soothe him with gentle words and one man held him gently on his lap. The older gentleman gave him a lemon drop candy to suck on.

While the men had their heated discussion with Miss Carmichael, Henry snuck into the house. Up the narrow creaking stairs and into his room.

I tiptoed silently into his room and tucked him in and smoothed his hair and softly hummed to him. When he was able to relax and fall asleep, I returned to my room.

The house was quiet but it took me a long time to settle enough to sleep.

Chapter 14

The board of directors had been informed of the incident concerning Henry. They paid a visit and extensively questioned Miss Carmichael for hours. After much discussion, sometimes heated, Miss Carmichael reassured them that it was an accident. That one of the younger children must have locked it not knowing someone was in there.

A Colonel Stewart listened with a skeptical look in his hazel eyes, hidden behind round frame glasses. He smoothed his greying moustache with his stout fingers, as he listened to Miss Carmichael. His brow creased as she attempted to explain the incidents of that day. He was a man of average height and build with a receding hairline.

After pondering over her ramblings, he politely requested to inspect the place. Miss Carmichael wrung her hands together and bit the corner of her lip. She appeared unwilling but hesitantly gave her consent.

The men thoroughly searched the house. They looked in the rooms, eyes flitting over threadbare, holey clothes hanging on nails. Their eyes widened in shock at the destitution and rundown neglected appearance of the place.

After the search, Colonel Stewart beckoned me aside and with a steady gaze inquired if we were treated kindly at the orphanage.

I opened my mouth to reply. Miss Carmichael gave me a look filled with pure evil, fists clenched by her sides, back ramrod straight, hate radiating off of her.

I will be beaten and locked up if I say anything, I thought, nausea filling my being, swallowing desperately in an attempt to keep it down. Goosebumps stood upright on my arms and shivers ran up and down my back. My heart pounded in my chest. I pressed my lips tightly together, remaining silent.

My hands were cold and clammy and I rubbed them with a jerky motion down my skirt. My chin dropped onto my chest and I squeezed my eyes closed. Trying to block the hate, I stood frozen in fear of her wrath.

He glanced quizzically at me, noticing my intense reaction. He then quickly glanced up at Miss Carmichael. Sharp awareness dawned in his eyes. He nodded brusquely. Colonel Stewart, his voice deep and soft, informed me that if I was in need, I was to come to him immediately.

I nodded my head slightly in acknowledgment. When he was leaving, he shook our hands. When he got to me, he slipped me a small piece of paper. I gazed up at him in astonishment. "It's my address," he mouthed and with a curt bow to Miss Carmichael, he strode from the room. The gentlemen left with promises to return periodically.

The house was quiet, and everyone was afraid to even breathe. We stood motionless.

Eyes fixed on Miss Carmichael. Miss Carmichael snorted angrily. She strode out of the room, her skirt swishing wildly around her ankles. We collectively breathed a silent sigh of relief.

Not long after this visit, a bright blue-eyed boy with a tangle of blonde curls moved in. He was an active lad with seemingly endless amounts of energy. At mealtimes, he couldn't sit still and tapped his feet or drummed his fingers on the table or mug. He would spill his drink or have other mishaps because of this. He chattered nonstop at the table and everywhere else. That was strictly not allowed, as children should be seen and not heard.

Miss Carmichael took an instant dislike for the boy. If he spoke, she backhanded him across the mouth. He would get whipped for no reason and locked in the basement for hours.

My eyes filled with tears as I saw him being dragged by the hair. Miss Carmichael berates him in angry tones. My heart was heavy. How could I free the children? What could I do? I needed a plan and I needed it soon.

Levi had been locked in the basement one late afternoon, when he was released, he was sullen and angry. His shoulders were slumped and he had a permanent scowl etched on his face.

A shot of fear ran through me, he looked like he had a bone to pick and would stop at nothing but revenge. I wanted to speak to him but I was locked in my room. I tried waving from the window, but his head was down and didn't notice.

Angrily he kicked a rock on the path. sailing into the tall grass by the trees. As he watched it soar, his face brightened. Stooping, he picked up a few small stones. Grinning, he dropped them into the pocket of his threadbare pants. He started whistling a jaunty tune as he purposefully meandered his way across the yard.

Immediately, I was suspicious. What has changed? He casually walked to the ancient oak tree, hoisting himself onto the nearest branch he nimbly swung his way up. Climbing quickly, he was hidden in the foliage. I could not see him from my bedroom window, I hoped that relaxing in the tree would calm him.

The breeze grew quiet, the leaves were still as if the world was holding her breath.

Waiting. Waiting for what?

I aimlessly wandered around my room. Brushing the dust off the dresser with my hand. With a bored expression, I glanced out the window.

I noticed Miss Carmichael casually walking by the tree, there was a slight rustling in the leaves, a branch swayed and dipped, and a hand burst forth from the tree's depth, it was clenching a rock! An impish face peers out and aims, the rock is released and it sails from the branches.

I gasped in horror as I watched it fly straight to the target. It smacks Miss Carmichael squarely on her left cheek instantly leaving a bright red mark.

Enraged she whirls around and glares up the tree demanding that Levi come down instantly.

Reaching up she grabs his foot. The branches wave wildly and Levi falls with a thud to the ground. Miss Carmichael with a death hold grabs his hair and shakes him. He trembles like a leaf in a thunderstorm.

The severity of his consequence's dawns on his pale features. Miss Carmichael hauls him by his hair, dragging him forcibly to the house.

Screaming at him, she informs him he was going straight to hell for his disrespect. She ranted on but I was unable to hear the tirade. I heard his screams of agony as loud thumps and whacks were heard hitting bare flesh.

I glanced around the yard, children cowering in fear. They are hunkered down behind shrubs, trees or the outhouse. The fear is visible, it is alive. The children cringe as they hear Levi's cries. Their eyes are wide in terror. Their thoughts were universal.

"Will I be next?"

After supper, I was allowed to leave my room. I wanted to see Levi, I could hear Miss Carmichael in the back of the house loudly disciplining a child. The children would be hiding from her. Cautiously, I glanced around, no one was in sight. Stealthily, I snuck down the stairs pausing to listen as the stair creaked. Silence. I was safe so far.

Levi was sitting in resigned silence, his hands shackled to the wall. His eye was swollen shut and was a deep purple. His face and body had large blue-black bruises and fire red welts covering him. The stick had further ripped his clothing and they were now in tatters. I gasped, my hand to my mouth, eyes wide in horror. This was the worst damage she had done yet.

Ignoring my reaction, he immediately informed me that he did not regret his actions, vehemently stating that Miss Carmichael was a very wicked woman. He raged about her evils.

I silently agreed with his assessment of her.

Trying to be of courage to him, I gently rubbed his back but he groaned in pain as my hand touched him. I withdrew my hands, not wanting to cause more pain. I wanted to believe that things would get better. I did not know what to say so I said nothing.

"Would someone have to die before there was a change?" I pondered morosely. Things have gotten so bad, what next? I remembered Mrs. Humiston had told me that bad times don't last forever but at what cost? I crossed my fingers behind my back and prayed it was true.

Levi shifted on the hard floor wincing in pain but remained stoic. His wounds looked so painful and he was so young. He couldn't be older than nine.

After promising to bring ointment for his sores, I slowly returned upstairs my heart heavy with sadness.

Listening to doorways so as not to be caught by Miss Carmichael, I heard her in the kitchen. She was glancing about the room as if to make sure she was alone. I eased back not wanting to be seen. When I believed it was safe, I peeked around the corner. She was opening a locked cupboard and pulled out a box.

I could not see it clearly but thought it may be the rat poison box. Why did she need that? There were no rats around here that I knew of. My eyes widened as she reached for the blue tin mug. With horror, I watched her as she added powder from the box and measured a small amount and placed it in the mug. She stood there grim-faced stirring the liquid with venom. Her presence was dark and foreboding. She took the container and placed it in the cupboard, locking it behind her.

Picking up the mug, she headed purposefully to the basement. Her steps loud and determined echoed eerily where I stood.

My eyes widened in shock and my heart started thumping wildly. I was frozen to the floor. What was she doing? What would poison do to a child? If that is what he is. I became lightheaded as the house swirled around me. My stomach started to grumble and I raced outside, throwing up over the deck until I was empty. Then I dry heaved until I was weak and shaky from losing all the contents of my stomach. I collapsed helplessly on the grass, and slowly my strength returned to me.

Later that evening, I snuck down the stairs to give him ointment for his wounds. He was moaning and complained plaintively of cramps in his stomach. He violently vomited and had a bout of bloody diarrhea that he was unable to control. He started convulsing and his eyes rolled back as his body writhed on the floor. His hands and feet were still shackled.

Trembling, I went out to find Miss Carmichael. Fearing the worst, I courageously informed her of Levi's illness and was scared she would beat me for visiting him.

She begrudgingly agreed he could be transferred upstairs grumbling in her gravelly voice that this would not have happened if he had behaved the illness was a consequence of his behavior. I ignored her as Levi needed to be cared for now.

Lizzie noticing the predicament assisted me in transferring the boy to a spare bed. She brought me a pail of warm soapy water and a clean pair of pajamas.

We wiped him clean and talked in soothing tones when he vomited or his body shook with convulsions.

As we cleaned him up, I informed Lizzie of what I had observed Miss Carmichael do with the drink.

Lizzie's eyes widened and her mouth dropped her hand motionless for a moment. "She tried to kill him." She moaned in agony.

The awfulness of the act filled us with many mixed emotions. We worked in silence giving comfort to the sick boy, trying to give him peace in his last hours. Our thoughts are a turmoil of rage, pain and utter helplessness.

In the early morning hours as the sun peeked over the horizon and the rays kissed the land, Levi had his worst convulsion. When it was over he closed his blue eyes and breathed his final breath.

Lizzie and I wept as we cleaned him one last time. When finished we crashed, exhausted into our beds.

When we awoke hours later, the boys had dug a grave for Levi beside the house. They also had built a rough coffin.

That evening we had a graveside service for Levi.

Miss Carmichael spoke on the importance of obedience and Levi had passed away as a result of his sin.

I pondered this as I gazed at his still features. I was going to miss this lighthearted impulsive child. For a short time, he had made the orphanage a brighter place.

He was lowered into the grave and the makeshift coffin was covered in the dirt. I knew that it wasn't because of his sin that he had to die. I believed with all my heart that it was Miss Carmichael's actions that made him die.

"What a friend we have in Jesus, all our sins and grief to bear," I softly hummed as I left the gravesite. I grieved the loss of the boy. I knew that he was in a better place safe from the abuse. He was now happy and free running through the green meadows in heaven.

A quiet thought came to me that I needed to write to Mr. Stewart and inform him of what was going on at the homestead.

The next evening, I found a scrap of paper and I told Mr. Stewart in the letter, of the beatings, being shackled in the basement, not being fed regularly and not being allowed to attend school. I wrote about Levi's suspicious death and other atrocities that happened here. When it was written, I sighed a load off my mind. I would send it off tomorrow and maybe there would be some help.

Tucking the faded quilt around my shoulders, I drifted off the peaceful sleep. I had the assurance I had done the right thing.

Chapter 15

I delivered the letter the following morning to the mail carrier. Now I waited for a response, knowing that it would take a while for Mr. Stewart to receive the letter, I was desperate for change.

Spring slowly arrived after a long, cold, wearisome winter. Beautiful wildflowers lifted their colorful faces towards the azure blue skies, birds sang merrily as they soared in the fresh air or sat in their nest, in the trees. Baby animals toddled after their mothers on thin wobbly legs.

Richard, Lizzie's brother, was getting frustrated with the dire situation. Miss Carmichael had hired him, to help the children follow the rules, with physical force. He now desired to change his nasty ways and live a more peaceful life. To stop being a bully, a creator of problems to someone who fixed problems.

One evening, while visiting with Lizzie and me, Richard confided that their mother had taught him to be kind to others and not be mean or cruel. Their mother had never allowed fighting between them, encouraging them to always use kind words and actions.

As we visited, worried that we would be heard, I fearfully glanced around, my ears were keen to any noises of approaching children or worse yet Miss Carmichael herself. My head throbbed in pain because of the potential of being caught, my anxiety was high. So far it appeared that no one had noticed us as we hid in the basement. We figured it was the only safe place to meet as the children despised the place.

Richard mentioned the feelings of pain and anger when his father passed away suddenly in a hunting accident. He was unable to cry and the pain turned to bitterness as he observed his mother struggle to provide for the family.

"I hated when Mother cried at night," Richard said softly. "I was helpless to comfort her." He turned his head abruptly, his eyes red and eyelashes fluttered rapidly.

Lizzie quietly spoke of her feelings about the deep loss of her father. She had been her father's shadow and did whatever her father did. They had felt rejected when their mother had placed them in the orphanage.

During their time of reflection, my mind wandered back to the sadness I had felt when my mother passed and the anger that Pa took out on me. I suddenly realized that he had been grieving too. He must have felt overwhelmed by the responsibility of taking care of me by himself.

As the years flashed by, I marveled that I had been able to survive on the streets as a small child. The kindness of Miss Emma and Mr. Frank. The early days at the orphanage had been a lot of fun too. Skating, riding in the sleigh, all the outdoor activities and picnics.

With a start, I realized I was miles away in my thoughts. Forgetting to listen for approaching people, I peered into the dimness, my ears alert for footsteps, breathing a sigh of relief when met with silence save for Richard and Lizzie's hushed tones.

The conversation had taken a turn and now they were reminiscing about growing up on a farm. Richard talked about the old ram they had and one day when he had been in the sheep pen, he didn't notice the ram behind him and it bunted him into the dugout. The water had been murky green with algae and mud. Water bugs skimmed the surface.

"Mother was very disgusted with me coming to the door covered in all that slime." Richard snorted. "She made me scrub off at the pump outside." Richard and Lizzie laughed at the memory, their hands covering their mouths.

I listened in amazement as they spoke of riding cows and how Richard rode one out of the barn and the cow started leaping and twisting and he fell face-first into cow manure. "I think that was when Mother started turning grey," he stated with a smirk. "You were always good," he commented turning to Lizzie.

"No," she said reflectively, "I just don't like being dirty," and she giggled.

They spoke reverently of how their mother had dreamed of a better life for them. How after their father had passed, there wasn't enough food to eat. Richard mentioned again hearing his mother sob in the night hours in desperation wondering how to keep them fed.

"She was probably very lonely," they mused. Their parents had had a close, loving relationship.

How would she feel with the way their lives had turned out?

Richard felt strongly time came for him to leave and search for his mother. Informing us that after finding her he hoped to get a job as a ranch hand on a local ranch.

Lizzie wished him the courage to face the unknown, wondering how he planned to find her. Richard informed me that they had received a letter from their mother addressed from a place in Connecticut. Richard acknowledged that it was over two years old and they hadn't heard anything from her since. "She may have moved, I have no way of knowing why she hasn't written. I will find out what has happened to her." Richard said in a determined tone.

We made him promise that he would inform the townsfolk of our plight. He had agreed without hesitation.

"They need to know." His face was serious, his lips pressed into a thin line.

Richard stood before us a pathetic-looking figure, tall and gangly, his dirty blonde hair fell messily into his dark dove grey eyes. His arms were twig-like and the deformed arm hung limply by his side.

Lizzie hugged him and cried. Richard patted her back reassuringly and promised to return and free her from this place.

Richard snuck out silently one cool June night, sliding down from his bedroom window on a rope attached to the window frame. The moon was full and bright and led his way to the town.

Lizzie and I had wanted to give him food for his journey, but as everything was locked, we were unable to help. He did take some fresh vegetables from the garden. We prayed he would be safe and Miss Carmichael would not catch him.

The next day the board of directors and a few of the town leaders stormed in without warning. They interviewed the terrified children and thoroughly searched the house. They were horrified when they saw the shackles attached to the dungeon wall.

I had grown accustomed to the living conditions and it was an eye-opening experience to see the house and the children through the eyes of the board members.

The children's bruises brought tears to my eyes as I realized fully what we had suffered. Us orphans wore not much more than rags and were unwashed and covered in lice and bed bug bites.

The gentlemen appeared to be disturbed by the neglect and lack of care of the orphans. They contacted the police immediately.

The police officers quickly got a warrant for Miss Carmichael's arrest.

Rumor was that she was interrogated for hours in a small room and was arrested later that evening. She had been handcuffed and brought to the local jail.

"Now she knows how we felt when we were handcuffed to the wall," Lizzie had growled spitefully.

"Yes," I said with a wink and a lopsided grin, "Serves her right with how she treated us."

I giggled and Lizzie joined in as we imagined the stately, pious Miss Carmichael handcuffed.

Mr. Stewart confided that they had just received my letter in the mail a few days ago.

When discussing with the other board members the contents of my letter, a boy had come into town. He claimed he was from the orphanage.

"Truthfully," Mr. Stewart stated bluntly, "it was hard to believe. The orphanage was supposed to be an upstanding place and this bedraggled, weary boy with filthy clothing and a rank body odor couldn't possibly have been from there. He had rambled on about his sister, Lizzie Hutchinson and a Bella Hunter who had been forced to wear men's clothing. Children being shackled to the basement wall and a girl who had been forced to stand in one position for hours."

Richard had accomplished what he had set out to do. I smiled to myself in the dusky darkness of the carriage. His story lined up with the letter I had written. Things had changed. The rescue had arrived. The younger children were on their way to stay with folks in town until they could find something permanent. The older ones would leave in a few days.

I inhaled deeply and slowly exhaled letting the crisp June air fill my lungs relieved that the unpleasant chapter of my life was closing.

Richard was recovering at a local farm family. I heard that he was enjoying the farm life but was insistent on finding his mother. The family with whom he was living requested that he stay with them until he completely recovered his strength.

The change had arrived and we looked with courage and hope to the future.

Chapter 16

June was hot that year and heatwaves shimmered over the hills and valleys. The sky was a radiant blue splattered with fluffy white clouds. Birds sang merrily and the breeze whispered in the trees. The world seemed full of hope and the promise of a good future.

The Gettysburg Homestead had officially closed its doors. The remaining orphans found homes in Gettysburg or were transferred to other orphanages.

Mr. Bourns was fired in disgrace for embezzlement and mismanagement of the funds. He had used the Sunday School's money that was for the orphanage, for his personal use. The money from Mrs. Humiston's ambrotype he kept for himself. He lived comfortably on it.

Miss Carmichael's bail was set at $300. Her court day was June 11, 1876. She was charged with three counts of aggravated assault and battery. She was found guilty of one count. As she was female, she was only made to pay $20 plus court costs.

Miss Carmichael was told to leave town and never return. She had one last duty to fulfil and that was to bring Lizzie and me to our new homes. That was one long uncomfortable ride. The carriage was filled with icy anger radiating off of her.

Lizzie and I had been given the choice of where we wanted to live. I chose Mr. and Mrs. Stewart whom I had become quite fond of.

Lizzie chose a couple from Philadelphia who offered to let her stay with them. They were an older couple but seemed kind. Their children had married and left home.

As the Stewarts also lived in Philadelphia, we wanted to keep in touch. Mr. Stewart promised that he would make sure we did.

I now had beautiful dresses tailor-made for me in my closet. They fit perfectly, and also many accessories to go with them. My bed made of walnut wood was soft and high with a quilt on it stitched by Mrs. Stewart's mother. It was made with a star pattern in lovely shades of blue, green and yellow.

Mrs. Stewart's mother wished that I would call her grandmother as she had no grandchildren. She was such a gentle thoughtful soul that I eagerly agreed. I hugged her soft, plump body and kissed her wrinkled cheek. She had hugged me back, her faded blue eyes shone with tears and happiness.

The Stewarts promised me that I would get schooling. I was very enthused about that as I had missed so much already. I planned to study hard as my dream was to teach and give others a love for learning.

I was blessed, my future was filled with choices and potential. I was happy and I knew that whatever would come, by the grace of God, I could be filled with peace and joy. And I knew I would live happily ever.

Bella Hunter is based on a true story. She was orphaned at an early age and was found wandering the streets in Philadelphia where she was sent to the soldier's orphanage.

The Philadelphia Fire happened in 1865, there were thirty lives lost and a lot of damage to the city. The fire started in the petroleum sheds.

The Civil War was the worst war up to that time due to fatalities, illness and accidents. Father's fought against sons. Brothers against brothers. Women helped as nurses and many hid their identities and fought side by side with their men. Robert Lee surrendered to Ulysses S. Grant on April 9th, 1865, at the Appomattox courthouse.

Abraham Lincoln was assassinated on April 14, 1865, as he watched a play in the theatre. His killer was John Wilkes Booth who was a well-known actor. John Wilkes Booth was also assassinated. The others who conspired along with him had a public hanging.

Abraham's remains were delivered to his final resting place by train making stops in the cities. He is buried beside his son William Wallace Lincoln (Willie) who passed away in 1862 in his hometown of Springfield Illinois.

Rosa Carmichael's bail was $300 which is equivalent to approximately $6620.82 in 2022 funds. $20 is about $441.39.

The Gettysburg Homestead was eventually auctioned and the doors were permanently closed.

On the 8th instant there occurred the most terrible conflagration that has taken place in Philadel-Sophia since the great fire of 1850. The fire originated about 2:30 a.m., in Washington Street, near Ninth, where there was an open lot on which BLACKBURN & Co. had between two and three thousand barrels of petroleum stored on account of various owners. The flames starting here spread almost with the rapidity of an explosion through the yard. Says the Philadelphia Bulletin: "The blazing oil that escaped from the burning barrels poured over into Ninth Street and down to Federal, filling the entire street with a lake of fire, igniting the houses on both sides of Ninth Street for two squares and carrying devastation into Washington, Ellsworth, and Federal streets, both above and below Ninth Street.

"An eyewitness, who was upon the spot when the oil poured out flame as resembling a screw in its progress. It first whirled up Ninth Street, and then the fiery torrent rushed down the street for a distance of two squares, and then back again at the caprice of the wind, destroying all living things that came in its way, burning dwellings and their contents as though they were mere straw, and even splitting into fragments the paving-stones in the street with the intense heat. Fully five squares of houses, had they been placed in a row, we're on fire at once, and the scene was one to make the stoutest heart quail.

"People escaping from their blazing homes, with no covering but their night-clothe; parents seeking for their children, and terrified little ones looking for safety in the horrid turmoil, were all dreadful enough, but there were still more terrible scenes witnessed. Men, women, and children were roasted alive in the streets."

It is thought that eight persons were burned to death. One of the most thrilling incidents connected with the fire was the daring attempt made by Mr. FLEETWOOD, a fireman, to rescue a lady from her house, which was encircled by the flames. It is thus described by the Philadelphia Press:

"The burning oil, hissing and seething, came pouring down the street, and the house, from which eleven persons had been rescued but a moment before, was licked up by the red, fiery tongues of the demon of Destruction. At this time the brave FLEETWOOD was bearing in his strong arms the body, it is supposed, of Mrs. WARE or one of her daughters. His companions were driven back by the approach of the burning element, the increasing heat and stifling smoke. Almost at the same moment, the burning oil burst through the rear part of the house, and, flowing through the entry, all chances of escape were gone. The brave fireman endeavored to fight his way out, still holding the woman in his arms. He reached the front doorstep; it was a moment of horror; he leaped from the step, driven by the flow of burning oil through the house, but the flames closed around him; a groan and a shriek escaped the lips of the victims, and both fell to their death. His companions endeavored to rescue both, but it was impossible. Their crisped remains were found but a few feet distant from each other."

The loss from the fire is estimated at half a million. That portion of this loss, which falls to the poorest of the sufferers, will probably be made to them by the charitable citizens.